Gary Paulsen has sailed the Pacific and competed in the  gruelling 1,049-mile Iditarod dog-sled race across Alaska. He is the distinguished author of numerous books, from westerns to DIY, and has received great acclaim and many awards for his novels written for young people.

His lives with his family in New Mexico, USA.

Also available from Macmillan Children's Books

MILLIONS
Frank Cottrell Boyce

BOOTLEG
Alex Shearer

THE ANGEL FACTORY
Terence Blacker

JAKE'S TOWER
Elizabeth Laird

A LITTLE PIECE OF GROUND
Elizabeth Laird

THE GARBAGE KING
Elizabeth Laird

HATCHET
And
HATCHET: THE RETURN

Gary Paulsen

MACMILLAN CHILDREN'S BOOKS

Hatchet first published 1989 and
Hatchet: The Return first published 1992 as *The Return*
by Macmillan Children's Books

This edition published 2005 by Macmillan Children's Books
a division of Macmillan Publishers Limited
20 New Wharf Road, London N1 9RR
Basingstoke and Oxford
www.panmacmillan.com

Associated companies throughout the world

ISBN 0 330 43871 9

1 3 5 7 9 8 6 4 2

A CIP catalogue record for this book is available from
the British Library.

Typeset by Intype Libra Ltd
Printed and bound in Great Britain by Mackays of Chatham plc, Kent

HATCHET

To the students of the Hershey Middle School

ONE

Brian Robeson stared out of the window of the small plane at the endless green northern wilderness below. It was a small plane, a Cessna 406 – a bushplane – and the engine was so loud, so roaring and consuming and loud, that it ruined any chance of conversation.

Not that he had much to say. He was thirteen and the only passenger on the plane with a pilot named – what was it? – Jim or Jake or something, who was in his mid-forties and who had been silent as he worked to prepare for take-off. In fact since Brian had come to the small airport in Hampton, New York to meet the plane – driven by his mother – the pilot had spoken only five words to him.

'Get in the co-pilot's seat.'

Which Brian had done. They had taken off and that was the last of the conversation. There had been the initial excitement, of course. He had never flown in a single-engine plane before and to be sitting in the co-pilot's seat with all the controls right there in front of him, all the instruments in his face as the plane clawed for altitude, jerking and sliding on the wind currents as the pilot took off, had been interesting and exciting. But in five minutes they had levelled off at six thousand feet and headed north-west and from then on the pilot had been silent, staring out of the front, and the drone of the engine

1

had been all that was left. The drone and the sea of green trees that lay before the plane's nose and flowed to the horizon, spread with lakes, swamps and wandering streams and rivers.

Now Brian sat, looking out of the window with the roar thundering through his ears, and tried to catalogue what had led up to his taking this flight.

The thinking started.

Always it started with a single word.

Divorce.

It was an ugly word, he thought. A tearing, ugly word that meant fights and yelling, lawyers – God, he thought, how he hated lawyers who sat with their comfortable smiles and tried to explain to him in legal terms how all that he lived in was coming apart – and the breaking and shattering of all the solid things. His home, his life – all the solid things. Divorce. A breaking word, an ugly breaking word.

Divorce.

Secrets.

No, not secrets so much as just the Secret. What he knew and had not told anybody, what he knew about his mother that had caused the divorce, what he knew, what he knew – the Secret.

Divorce.

The Secret.

Brian felt his eyes beginning to burn and knew there would be tears. He had cried for a time, but that was gone now. He didn't cry now. Instead his eyes burned and tears came, the seeping tears that burned, but he didn't cry. He wiped his eyes with a finger and looked at the pilot out of the corner of his eye to make sure he hadn't noticed the burning and tears.

The pilot sat large, his hands lightly on the wheel, feet on the rudder pedals. He seemed more a machine than a man, an extension of the plane. On the dashboard in front of him Brian saw dials, switches, meters, knobs, levers, cranks, lights, handles that were wiggling and flickering, all indicating nothing that he understood, and the pilot seemed the same way. Part of the plane, not human.

When he saw Brian look at him, the pilot seemed to open up a bit and he smiled. 'Ever fly in the co-pilot's seat before?' He leaned over and lifted the headset off his right ear and put it on his temple, yelling to overcome the sound of the engine.

Brian shook his head. He had never been in any kind of plane, never seen the cockpit of a plane except in films or on television. It was loud and confusing. 'First time.'

'It's not as complicated as it looks. Good plane like this almost flies itself.' The pilot shrugged. 'Makes my job easy.' He took Brian's left arm. 'Here, put your hands on the controls, your feet on the rudder pedals, and I'll show you what I mean.'

Brian shook his head, 'I'd better not.'

'Sure. Try it . . .'

Brian reached out and took the wheel in a grip so tight his knuckles were white. He pushed his feet down on the pedals. The plane slewed suddenly to the right.

'Not so hard. Take her light, take her light.'

Brian eased off, relaxed his grip. The burning in his eyes was forgotten momentarily as the vibration of the plane came through the wheel and the pedals. It seemed almost alive.

'See?' The pilot let go of his wheel, raised his hands

in the air and took his feet off the pedals to show Brian he was actually flying the plane alone. 'Simple. Now turn the wheel a little to the right and push on the right rudder pedal a small amount.'

Brian turned the wheel slightly and the plane immediately banked to the right, and when he pressed on the right rudder pedal the nose slid across the horizon to the right. He left off on the pressure and straightened the wheel and the plane righted itself.

'Now you can turn. Bring her back to the left a little.'

Brian turned the wheel left, pushed on the left pedal, and the plane came back round. 'It's easy.' He smiled. 'At least this part.'

The pilot nodded. 'All of flying is easy. Just takes learning. Like everything else. Like everything else.' He took the controls back, then reached up and rubbed his left shoulder. 'Aches and pains – must be getting old.'

Brian let go of the controls and moved his feet away from the pedals as the pilot put his hands on the wheel. 'Thank you . . .'

But the pilot had put his headset back on and the gratitude was lost in the engine noise and things went back to Brian looking out of the window at the ocean of trees and lakes. The burning eyes did not come back, but memories did, came flooding in. The words. Always the words.

Divorce.

The Secret.

Fights.

Split.

The big split. Brian's father did not understand as Brian did, knew only that Brian's mother wanted to break the marriage apart. The split had come and then the divorce, all so fast, and the court had left him with his mother except for the summers and what the judge called 'visitation rights'. So formal. Brian hated judges as he hated lawyers. Judges who leaned over the bench and asked Brian if he understood where he was to live and why. Judges who did not know what had really happened. Judges with the caring look that meant nothing as lawyers said legal phrases that meant nothing.

In the summer Brian would live with his father. In the school year with his mother. That's what the judge said after looking at papers on his desk and listening to the lawyers talk. Talk. Words.

Now the plane lurched slightly to the right and Brian looked at the pilot. He was rubbing his shoulder again and there was the sudden smell of body gas in the plane. Brian turned back to avoid embarrassing the pilot, who was obviously in some discomfort. Must have stomach trouble.

So this summer, this first summer that he was allowed to have 'visitation rights' with his father, with the divorce only one month old, Brian was heading north. His father was a mechanical engineer who had designed or invented a new drill bit for oil drilling, a self-cleaning, self-sharpening bit. He was working in the oil fields of Canada, up on the tree line where the tundra started and the forests ended. Brian was flying up from New York with some drilling equipment – it was lashed down in the rear of the plane next to a fabric bag the pilot had called a survival pack, which had emergency supplies in case they had to make an emergency landing – that had to be specially made in the city, flying in a bushplane with the pilot named Jim or Jake or something who had turned out to be an all right guy, letting him fly and all.

Except for the smell. Now there was a constant odour, and Brian took another look at the pilot, found him rubbing the shoulder and down the arm now, the left arm, letting go more gas and wincing. Probably something he ate, Brian thought.

His mother had driven him from the city to meet the plane at Hampton where it came to pick up the drilling equipment. A drive in silence, a long drive in silence. Two and a half hours of sitting in the car, staring out of the window just as he was now staring out of the window of the plane. Once, after an hour, when they were out of the city, she turned to him.

'Look, can't we talk this over? Can't we talk this out? Can't you tell me what's bothering you?'

And there were the words again. Divorce. Split. The Secret. How could he tell her what he knew? So he had remained silent, shook his head and continued to stare unseeing at the countryside, and his mother had gone back to driving only to speak to him one more time when they were close to Hampton.

She reached over the back of the seat and brought up a paper bag. 'I got something for you, for the trip.'

Brian took the bag and opened the top. Inside there was a hatchet, the kind with a steel handle and a rubber handgrip. The head was in a stout leather case that had a brass-riveted belt loop.

'It goes on your belt.' His mother spoke without looking at him. There were some farm trucks on the road now and she had to weave through them and watch the traffic. 'The man at the shop said you could use it. You know. In the woods with your father.'

Dad, he thought. Not 'my father'. My dad. 'Thanks. It's really nice.' But the words sounded hollow, even to Brian.

'Try it on. See how it looks on your belt.'

And he would normally have said no, would normally have said that it looked too naff to have a hatchet on your belt. Those were the normal things he would say. But her voice was thin, had a sound like something thin that would break if you touched it, and he felt bad for not speaking to her. Knowing what he knew, even with the anger, the hot white hate of his anger at her, he still felt bad for not speaking to her, and so to humour her he loosened his belt and pulled the right side out and put the hatchet on and rethreaded the belt.

'Scootch round so I can see.'

He moved round in the seat, feeling only slightly ridiculous.

She nodded. 'Just like a scout. My little scout.' And there was the tenderness in her voice that she had when he was small, the tenderness that she had when he was small and sick, with a cold, and she put her hand on his forehead, and the burning came into his eyes again and he had turned away from her and looked out of the window, forgotten the hatchet and so arrived at the plane with the hatchet still on his belt.

Because it was a bush flight from a small airport there had been no security and the plane had been waiting with the engine running when he arrived and he had grabbed his suitcase and pack bag and run for the plane without stopping to remove the hatchet.

So it was still on his belt. At first he had been embarrassed but the pilot had said nothing about it and Brian forgot it as they took off and began flying.

More smell now. Bad. Brian turned again to glance at the pilot, who had both hands on his stomach and was grimacing in pain, reaching for the left shoulder again as Brian watched.

'Don't know, kid . . .' The pilot's words were a hiss, barely audible. 'Bad aches. Thought it was something I ate but . . .'

He stopped as a fresh spasm of pain hit him. Even Brian could see how bad it was – the pain drove the pilot back into the seat, back and down.

'I've never had anything like this . . .'

The pilot reached for the switch on his mike cord, his hand coming up in a small arc from his stomach, and he flipped the switch and said, 'This is flight four six . . .'

And now a jolt took him like a hammer blow, so forcefully that he seemed to crush back into the seat, and Brian reached for him, could not understand at first what it was, could not know.

And then knew.

Brian knew. The pilot's mouth went rigid, he swore and jerked a short series of slams into the seat, holding his shoulder now. Swore and hissed, 'Chest! Oh God, my chest is coming apart!'

Brian knew now.

The pilot was having a heart attack. Brian had been in the shopping mall with his mother when a man in front of Paisley's store had suffered a heart attack. He had gone down and screamed about his chest. An old man. Much older than than the pilot.

Brian knew.

8

The pilot was having a heart attack and even as the knowledge came to Brian he saw the pilot slam into the seat one more time, one more awful time he slammed back into the seat and his right leg jerked, pulling the plane to the side in a sudden twist, and his head fell forward and spit came. Spit came from the corners of his mouth and his legs contracted up, up into the seat, and his eyes rolled back in his head until there was only white.

Only white for his eyes and the smell became worse, filled the cockpit, and all of it so fast, so incredibly fast that Brian's mind could not take it in at first. Could only see it in stages.

The pilot had been talking, just a moment ago, complaining of the pain. He had been talking.

Then the jolts had come.

The jolts that took the pilot back had come, and now Brian sat and there was a strange feeling of silence in the thrumming roar of the engine – a strange feeling of silence and being alone. Brian was stopped.

He was stopped. Inside he was stopped. He could not think past what he saw, what he felt. All was stopped. The very core of him, the very centre of Brian Robeson was stopped and stricken with a white-flash of horror, a terror so intense that his breathing, his thinking, and nearly his heart had stopped.

Stopped.

Seconds passed, seconds that became all of his life, and he began to know what he was seeing, began to understand what he saw and that was worse, so much worse that he wanted to make his mind freeze again.

He was sitting in a bushplane roaring seven thousand feet above the northern wilderness with a pilot who had suffered a massive heart attack and who was either dead or in something close to a coma.

He was alone.

In the roaring plane with no pilot he was alone.

Alone.

TWO

For a time that he could not understand Brian could do nothing. Even after his mind began working and he could see what had happened he could do nothing. It was as if his hands and arms were lead.

Then he looked for ways for it not to have happened. Be asleep, his mind screamed at the pilot. Just be asleep and your eyes will open now and your hands will take the controls and your feet will move to the pedals – but it did not happen.

The pilot did not move except that his head rolled on a neck impossibly loose as the plane hit a small bit of turbulence.

The plane.

Somehow the plane was still flying. Seconds had passed, nearly a minute, and the plane flew on as if nothing had happened and he had to do something, had to do something but did not know what.

Help.

He had to help.

He stretched one hand toward the pilot, saw that his fingers were trembling, and touched the pilot on the chest. He did not know what to do. He knew there were procedures, that you could do mouth-to-mouth on victims of heart attacks and push their chests, but he did not know how to do it and in any case could not do it with the pilot, who was sitting up in the seat and still strapped in with his seatbelt.

So he touched the pilot with the tips of his fingers, touched him on the chest and could feel nothing, no heartbeat, no rise and fall of breathing. Which meant that the pilot was almost certainly dead.

'Please,' Brian said. But did not know what or who to ask. 'Please . . .'

The plane lurched again, hit more turbulence, and Brian felt the nose drop. It did not dive, but the nose went down slightly and the down-angle increased the speed, and he knew that at this angle, this slight angle down, he would ultimately fly into the trees. He could see them ahead on the horizon where before he could see only sky.

He had to fly it somehow. Had to fly the plane. He had to help himself. The pilot was gone, beyond anything he could do. He had to try and fly the plane.

He turned back in the seat, facing the front, and put his hands – still trembling – on the control wheel, his feet gently on the rudder pedals. You pulled back on the stick to raise the plane, he knew that from reading. You always pulled back on the wheel. He gave it a tug and it slid back toward him easily. Too easily. The plane, with the increased speed from the tilt down, swooped eagerly up and drove Brian's stomach down. He pushed the wheel back in, went too far this time, and the plane's nose went below the horizon and the engine speed increased with the shallow dive.

Too much.

He pulled back again, more gently this time, and the nose floated up again, too far but not as violently as before, then down a bit too much, and up again very easily, and the front of the engine cowling settled. When he had it aimed at the horizon and it

12

seemed to be steady, he held the wheel where it was, let out his breath – which he had been holding all this time – and tried to think what to do next.

It was a clear, blue-sky day with fluffy bits of clouds here and there and he looked out of the window for a moment, hoping to see something, a town or village, but there was nothing. Just the green of the trees, endless green, and lakes scattered more and more thickly as the plane flew – where?

He was flying but did not know where, had no idea where he was going. He looked at the dashboard of the plane, studied the dials and hoped to get some help, hoped to find a compass, but it was all so confusing, a jumble of numbers and lights. One lighted display in the top centre of the dashboard said the number 342, another next to it said 22. Down beneath that were dials with lines that seemed to indicate what the wings were doing, tipping or moving, and one dial with a needle pointing to the number 70, which he thought – only thought – might be the altimeter. The device that told him his height above the ground. Or above sea level. Somewhere he had read something about altimeters but he couldn't remember what, or where, or anything about them.

Slightly to the left and below the altimeter he saw a small rectangular panel with a lighted dial and two knobs. His eyes had passed over it two or three times before he saw what was written in tiny letters on top of the panel. TRANSMITTER 221 was stamped in the metal and it hit him, finally, that this was the radio.

The radio. Of course. He had to use the radio. When the pilot had – had been hit that way (he couldn't bring himself to say that the pilot was dead, couldn't think it), he had been trying to use the radio.

Brian looked at the pilot. The headset was still on his head, turned sideways a bit from his jamming back into the seat, and the microphone switch was clipped into his belt.

Brian had to get the headset from the pilot. Had to reach over and get the headset from the pilot or he would not be able to use the radio to call for help. He had to reach over . . .

His hands began trembling again. He did not want to touch the pilot, did not want to reach for him. But he had to. Had to get the radio. He lifted his hands from the wheel, just slightly, and held them waiting to see what would happen. The plane flew on normally, smoothly.

All right, he thought. Now. Now to do this thing. He turned and reached for the headset, slid it from the pilot's head, one eye on the plane, waiting for it to dive. The headset came easily, but the microphone switch at the pilot's belt was jammed in and he had to pull to get it loose. When he pulled, his elbow bumped the wheel and pushed it in and the plane started down in a shallow dive. Brian grabbed the wheel and pulled it back, too hard again, and the plane went through another series of stomach-wrenching swoops up and down before he could get it under control.

When things had settled again he pulled at the mike cord once more and at last jerked the cord free. It took him another second or two to place the headset on his own head and position the small microphone tube in front of his mouth. He had seen the pilot use it, had seen him depress the switch at

14

his belt, so Brian pushed the switch in and blew into the mike.

He heard the sound of his breath in the headset. 'Hello! Is there anybody listening on this? Hello . . .'

He repeated it two or three times and then waited but heard nothing except his own breathing.

Panic came then. He had been afraid, had been stopped with the terror of what was happening, but now panic came and he began to scream into the microphone, scream over and over.

'Help! Somebody help me! I'm in this plane and don't know . . . don't know . . . don't know . . .'

And he started crying with the screams, crying and slamming his hands against the wheel of the plane, causing it to jerk down, then back up. But again, he heard nothing but the sound of his own sobs in the microphone, his own screams mocking him, coming back into his ears.

The microphone. Awareness cut into him. He had used a CB radio in his uncle's pick-up truck once. You had to turn the mike switch off to hear anybody else. He reached to his belt and released the switch.

For a second all he heard was the *whusssh* of the empty air waves. Then, through the noise and static he heard a voice.

'Whoever is calling on this radio net, I repeat, release your mike switch – you are covering me. You are covering me. Over.'

It stopped and Brian hit his mike switch. 'I hear you! I hear you. This is me . . .!' He released the switch.

'Roger, I have you now.' The voice was very faint and breaking up. 'Please state your difficulty and location. And say *over* to signal end of transmission. Over.'

Please state my difficulty, Brian thought. God. My difficulty. 'I am in a plane with a pilot who is – who has had a heart attack or something. He is – he can't fly. And I don't know how to fly. Help me. Help . . .' He turned his mike off without ending transmission properly.

There was a moment's hesitation before the answer. 'Your signal is breaking up and I lost most of it. Understand . . . pilot . . . you can't fly. Correct? Over.'

Brian could barely hear him now, heard mostly noise and static. 'That's right. I can't fly. The plane is flying now but I don't know how much longer. Over.'

' . . . lost signal. Your location please. Flight number . . . location . . . ver.'

'I don't know my flight number or location. I don't know anything. I told you that, over.'

He waited now, waited but there was nothing. Once, for a second, he thought he heard a break in the noise, some part of a word, but it could have been static. Two, three minutes, ten minutes, the plane roared and Brian listened but heard no one. Then he hit the switch again.

'I do not know the flight number. My name is Brian Robeson and we left Hampton, New York headed for the Canadian oil fields to visit my father and I do not know how to fly an aeroplane and the pilot . . .'

He let go of the mike. His voice was starting to rattle and he felt as if he might start screaming at any second. He took a deep breath. 'If there is anybody listening who can help me fly a plane, please answer.'

Again he released the mike but heard nothing but

the hissing of noise in the headset. After half an hour of listening and repeating the cry for help he tore the headset off in frustration and threw it to the floor. It all seemed so hopeless. Even if he did get somebody, what could anybody do? Tell him to be careful?

All so hopeless.

He tried to figure out the dials again. He thought he might know which was speed – it was a lighted number that read 160 – but he didn't know if that was actual miles an hour, or kilometres, or if it just meant how fast the plane was moving through the air and not over the ground. He knew airspeed was different from groundspeed but not by how much.

Parts of books he'd read about flying came to him. How wings worked, how the propeller pulled the plane through the sky. Simple things that wouldn't help him now.

Nothing could help him now.

An hour passed. He picked up the headset and tried again – it was, he knew, in the end all he had – but there was no answer. He felt like a prisoner, kept in a small cell that was hurtling through the sky at what he thought to be 160 miles an hour, headed – he didn't know where – just headed somewhere until . . .

There it was. Until what? Until he ran out of fuel. When the plane ran out of fuel it would go down.

Period.

Or he could pull the throttle out and make it go down now. He had seen the pilot push the throttle in to increase speed. If he pulled the throttle back out, the engine would slow down and the plane would go down.

Those were his choices. He could wait for the plane

17

to run out of fuel and fall or he could push the throttle in and make it happen sooner. If he waited for the plane to run out of fuel he would go further – but he did not know which way he was moving. When the pilot had jerked he had moved the plane, but Brian could not remember how much or if it had come back to its original course. Since he did not know the original course anyway and could only guess at which display might be the compass – the one reading 342 – he did not know where he had been or where he was going, so it didn't make much difference if he went down now or waited.

Everything in him rebelled against stopping the engine and falling now. He had a vague feeling that he was wrong to keep heading as the plane was heading, a feeling that he might be going off in the wrong direction, but he could not bring himself to stop the engine and fall. Now he was safe, or safer than if he went down – the plane was flying, he was still breathing. When the engine stopped he would go down.

So he left the plane running, holding altitude, and kept trying the radio. He worked out a system. Every ten minutes by the small clock built into the dashboard he tried the radio with a simple message: 'I need help. Is there anybody listening to me?'

In the times between transmissions he tried to prepare himself for what he knew was coming. When he ran out of fuel the plane would start down. He guessed that without the propeller pulling he would have to push the nose down to keep the plane flying – he thought he may have read that somewhere, or it just came to him. Either way it made sense. He would have to push the nose down to keep flying speed and then, just before he hit, he would have to pull the nose back up to slow the plane as much as possible.

It all made sense. Glide down, then slow the plane and hit.

Hit.

He would have to find a clearing as he went down. The problem with that was he hadn't seen one clearing since they'd started flying over the forest. Some swamps, but they had trees scattered through them. No roads, no trails, no clearings.

Just the lakes, and it came to him that he would have to use a lake for landing. If he went down in the trees he was certain to die. The trees would tear the plane to pieces as it went into them.

He would have to come down in a lake. No. On the edge of a lake. He would have to come down near the edge of a lake and try to slow the plane as much as possible just before he hit the water.

Easy to say, he thought, hard to do.

Easy say, hard do. Easy say, hard do. It became a chant that beat with the engine. Easy say, hard do.

Impossible to do.

He repeated the radio call seventeen times at the ten-minute intervals, working on what he would do between transmissions. Once more he reached over to the pilot and touched him on the face, but the skin was cold, hard cold, death cold, and Brian turned back to the dashboard. He did what he could, tightened his seatbelt, positioned himself, rehearsed mentally again and again what his procedure should be.

When the plane ran out of fuel he should hold the nose down and head for the nearest lake and try to fly the plane kind of on to the water. That's how he thought of it. Kind of fly the plane on to the water. And just before it hit he should pull back on the wheel and slow the plane down to reduce the impact.

Over and over his mind ran the picture of how it would go. The plane running out of fuel, flying the plane on to the water, the crash – from pictures he'd seen on television. He tried to visualise it. He tried to be ready.

But between the seventeenth and eighteenth radio transmissions, without a warning, the engine coughed, roared violently for a second and died. There was sudden silence, cut only by the sound of the windmilling propeller and the wind past the cockpit.

Brian pushed the nose of the plane down and threw up.

THREE

Going to die, Brian thought. Going to die, gonna die, gonna die – his whole brain screamed it in the sudden silence.

Gonna die.

He wiped his mouth with the back of his arm and held the nose down. The plane went into a glide, a very fast glide that ate altitude, and suddenly there weren't any lakes. All he'd seen since they started flying over the forest was lakes and now they were gone. Gone. Out in front, far away at the horizon, he could see lots of them, off to the right and left more of them, glittering blue in the late afternoon sun.

But he needed one right in front. He desperately needed a lake right in front of the plane and all he saw through the windscreen were trees, green death trees. If he had to turn – if he had to turn he didn't think he could keep the plane flying. His stomach tightened into a series of rolling knots and his breath came in short bursts . . .

There!

Not quite in front but slightly to the right he saw a lake. L-shaped, with rounded corners, and the plane was nearly aimed at the long part of the L, coming from the bottom and heading to the top. Just a tiny bit to the right. He pushed the right rudder pedal gently and the nose moved over.

But the turn cost him speed and now the lake was above the nose. He pulled back on the wheel slightly and the nose came up. This caused the plane to slow dramatically and almost seem to stop and wallow in the air. The controls became very loose-feeling and frightened Brian, making him push the wheel back in. This increased the speed a bit but filled the windscreen once more with nothing but trees, and put the lake well above the nose and out of reach.

For a space of three or four seconds things seemed to hang, almost to stop. The plane was flying, but so slowly, so slowly . . . it would never reach the lake. Brian looked out to the side and saw a small pond and at the edge of the pond some large animal – he thought a moose – standing out in the water. All so still looking, so stopped, the pond and the moose and the trees, as he slid over them now only three or four hundred feet off the ground – all like a picture.

Then everything happened at once. Trees suddenly took on detail, filled his whole field of vision with green, and he knew he would hit and die, would die, but his luck held and just as he was to hit he came into an open lane, a channel of fallen trees, a wide place leading to the lake.

The plane, committed now to landing, to crashing, fell into the wide place like a stone, and Brian eased back on the wheel and braced himself for the crash. But there was a tiny bit of speed left and when he pulled on the wheel the nose came up and he saw in front the blue of the lake and at that instant the plane hit the trees.

There was a great wrenching as the wings caught the pines at the side of the clearing and broke back, ripping back just outside the main braces. Dust and dirt blew off the floor into his face so hard he thought there must have been some kind of explosion. He was momentarily blinded and slammed forward in the seat, smashing his head on the wheel.

Then a wild crashing sound, ripping of metal, and the plane rolled to the right and blew through the trees, out over the water and down, down to slam into the lake, skip once on water as hard as concrete, water that tore the windscreen out and shattered the side windows, water that drove him back into the seat. Somebody was screaming, screaming as the plane drove down into the water. Someone screamed tight animal screams of fear and pain and he did not know that it was his sound, that he roared against the water that took him and the plane still deeper, down in the water. He saw nothing but sensed blue, cold blue-green, and he raked at the seatbelt catch, tore his nails loose on one hand. He ripped at it until it released and somehow – the water trying to kill him, to end him – somehow he pulled himself out of the shattered front window and clawed up into the blue, felt something hold him back, felt his anorak tear and he was free. Tearing free. Ripping free.

But so far! So far to the surface and his lungs could not do this thing, could not hold and were through, and he sucked water, took a great pull of water that would – finally – win, finally take him, and his head broke into light and he vomited and swam, pulling without knowing what he was, what he was doing. Without knowing anything. Pulling until his hands caught at weeds and muck, pulling and screaming until his hands caught at last in grass and brush and he felt his chest on land, felt his face in the coarse blades of grass and he stopped, everything stopped.

A colour came that he had never seen before, a colour that exploded in his mind with the pain and he was gone, gone from it all, spiralling out into the world, spiralling out into nothing.

Nothing.

FOUR

The memory was like a knife cutting into him. Slicing deep into him with hate.

The Secret.

He had been riding his ten-speed with a friend named Terry. They had been taking a run on a bike trail and decided to come back a different way, a way that took them past the Amber Mall. Brian remembered everything in incredible detail. Remembered the time on the bank clock in the mall, flashing 3:31, then the temperature, 82, and the date. All the numbers were part of the memory, all of his life was part of the memory.

Terry had just turned to smile at him about something and Brian looked over Terry's head and saw her.

His mother.

She was sitting in a car, a strange car. He saw her and she did not see him. Brian was going to wave or call out, but something stopped him. There was a man in the car.

Short blond hair, the man had. Wearing some kind of white tennis shirt.

Brian saw this and more, saw the Secret and saw more later, but the memory came in pieces, came in scenes like this – Terry smiling, Brian looking over his head to see the car and his mother sitting with the man, the time and temperature clock, the front

25

wheel of his bike, the short blond hair of the man, the white shirt of the man, the hot-hate slices of the memory were exact.

The Secret.

Brian opened his eyes and screamed.

For seconds he did not know where he was, only that the crash was still happening and he was going to die, and he screamed until his breath was gone.

Then silence, filled with sobs as he pulled in air, half crying. How could it be so quiet? Moments ago there was nothing but noise, crashing and tearing, screaming, now quiet.

Some birds were singing.

How could birds be singing?

His legs felt wet and he raised himself up on his hands and looked back down at them. They were in the lake. Strange. They went down into the water. He tried to move, but pain hammered into him and made his breath shorten into gasps and he stopped, his legs still in the water.

Pain.

Memory.

He turned again and sun came across the water, late sun, cut into his eyes and made him turn away.

It was over then. The crash.

He was alive.

The crash is over and I am alive, he thought. Then his eyes closed and he lowered his head for minutes that seemed longer. When he opened them again it was evening and some of the sharp pain had abated – there were many dull aches – and the crash came back to him fully.

Into the trees and out on to the lake. The plane

had crashed and sunk in the lake and he had somehow pulled free.

He raised himself and crawled out of the water, grunting with the pain of movement. His legs were on fire, and his forehead felt as if somebody had been pounding on it with a hammer, but he could move. He pulled his legs out of the lake and crawled on his hands and knees until he was away from the wet-soft shore and near a clump of brush of some kind.

Then he went down, only this time to rest, to save something of himself. He lay on his side and put his head on his arm and closed his eyes because that was all he could do now, all he could think of being able to do. He closed his eyes and slept, dreamless, deep and down.

There was almost no light when he opened his eyes again. The darkness of night was thick and for a moment he began to panic again. To see, he thought. To see is everything. And he could not see. But he turned his head without moving his body and saw that across the lake the sky was a light grey, that the sun was starting to come up, and he remembered that it had been evening when he went to sleep.

'Must be morning now . . .' He mumbled it, almost in a hoarse whisper. As the thickness of sleep left him the world came back.

He was still in pain, all-over pain. His legs were cramped and drawn up, tight and aching, and his back hurt when he tried to move. Worst was a keening throb in his head that pulsed with every beat of his heart. It seemed that the whole crash had happened to his head.

He rolled on his back and felt his sides and his legs,

27

moving things slowly. He rubbed his arms; nothing seemed to be shattered or even sprained all that badly. When he was nine he had ploughed his small dirt bike into a parked car and broken his ankle, had to wear a cast for eight weeks, and there was nothing now like that. Nothing broken. Just battered around a bit.

His forehead felt massively swollen to the touch, almost like a mound out over his eyes, and it was so tender that when his fingers grazed it he nearly cried. But there was nothing he could do about it and, like the rest of him, it seemed to be bruised more than broken.

I'm alive, he thought. I'm alive. It could have been different. There could have been death. I could have been done.

Like the pilot, he thought suddenly. The pilot in the plane, down into the water, down into the blue water strapped in the seat . . .

He sat up – or tried to. The first time he fell back. But on the second attempt, grunting with the effort, he managed to come to a sitting position and scrunched sideways until his back was against a small tree where he sat facing the lake, watching the sky get lighter and lighter with the coming dawn.

His clothes were wet and clammy and there was a faint chill. He pulled the torn remnants of his anorak, pieces really, around his shoulders and tried to hold what heat his body could find. He could not think, could not make thought patterns work right. Things seemed to go back and forth between reality and imagination – except that it was all reality. One second he seemed only to have imagined that there was a plane crash, that he had fought out of the sinking plane and swum to shore; that it had all happened to some other person or in a film playing in his mind. Then he would feel his clothes, wet and cold, and his forehead would slash a pain through his thoughts and he would know it was real, that it had really happened. But all in a haze, all in a haze-world. So he sat and stared at the lake, felt the pain come and go in waves, and watched the sun come over the end of the lake.

It took an hour, perhaps two – he could not measure time yet and didn't care – for the sun to get halfway up. With it came some warmth, small bits of it at first, and with the heat came clouds of insects – thick, swarming hordes of mosquitoes that flocked to his body, made a living coat on his exposed skin, clogged his nostrils when he inhaled, poured into his mouth when he opened it to take a breath.

It was not possibly believable. Not this. He had come through the crash, but the insects were not possible. He coughed them up, spat them out, sneezed them out, closed his eyes and kept brushing his face, slapping and crushing them by the dozens, by the hundreds. But as soon as he cleared a place, as soon as he killed them, more came, thick, whining, buzzing masses of them. Mosquitoes and some small black flies he had never seen before. All biting, chewing, taking from him.

In moments his eyes were swollen shut and his face puffy and round to match his battered forehead. He pulled the torn pieces of his anorak over his head and tried to shelter in it but the jacket was full of rips and it didn't work. In desperation he pulled his T-shirt up to cover his face, but that exposed the skin of his lower back and the mosquitoes and flies attacked the new soft flesh of his back so viciously that he pulled the shirt down.

In the end he sat with the anorak pulled up, brushed with his hands and took it, almost crying in frustration and agony. There was nothing left to do. And when the sun was fully up and heating him directly, bringing steam off his wet clothes and bathing him with warmth, the mosquitoes and flies disappeared. Almost that suddenly. One minute he was sitting in the middle of a swarm; the next, they were gone and the sun was on him.

Vampires, he thought. Apparently they didn't like the deep of night, perhaps because it was too cool, and they couldn't take the direct sunlight. But in that grey time in the morning, when it began to get warm and before the sun was full up and hot – he couldn't believe them. Never, in all the reading, in the films he had watched on television about the outdoors; never once had they mentioned the mosquitoes or flies. All they ever showed on the nature programmes was beautiful scenery or animals jumping around having a good time. Nobody ever mentioned mosquitoes and flies.

'Unnnhhh.' He pulled himself up to stand against the tree and stretched, bringing new aches and pains. His back muscles must have been hurt as well – they almost seemed to tear when he stretched – and while the pain in his forehead seemed to be abating somewhat, just trying to stand made him weak enough to nearly collapse.

The backs of his hands were puffy and his eyes were almost swollen shut from the mosquitoes, and he saw everything through a narrow squint.

Not that there was much to see, he thought, scrat-

30

ching the bites. In front of him lay the lake, blue and deep. He had a sudden picture of the plane, sunk in the lake, down and down in the blue with the pilot's body still strapped in the seat, his hair waving.

He shook his head. More pain. That wasn't something to think about.

He looked at his surroundings again. The lake stretched out slightly below him. He was at the base of the L, looking up the long part with the short part out to his right. In the morning light and calm the water was absolutely, perfectly still. He could see the reflections of the trees at the other end of the lake. Upside down in the water they seemed almost like another forest, an upside-down forest to match the real one. As he watched, a large bird – he thought it looked like a crow but it seemed larger – flew from the top, real forest, and the reflection-bird matched it, both flying out over the water.

Everything was green, so green it went into him. The forest was largely made up of pines and spruce, with clumps of some low brush smeared here and there and thick grass and some other kind of very small brush all over. He couldn't identify most of it, except the evergreens, and some leafy trees he thought might be aspen. He'd seen pictures of aspen in the mountains on television. The country around the lake was moderately hilly, but the hills were small – almost hummocks – and there were very few rocks except to his left. There lay a rocky ridge that stuck out overlooking the lake, about twenty feet high.

If the plane had come down a little to the left it would have hit the rocks and never made the lake. He would have been smashed.

Destroyed.

The word came. I would have been destroyed and torn and smashed. Driven into the rocks and destroyed.

Luck, he thought. I have luck, I had good luck there. But he knew that was wrong. If he had had good luck his parents wouldn't have divorced because of the Secret and he wouldn't have been flying with a pilot who had a heart attack and he wouldn't be here where he had to have good luck to keep from being destroyed.

If you keep walking back from good luck, he thought, you'll come to bad luck.

He shook his head again, wincing. Another thing not to think about.

The rocky ridge was rounded and seemed to be of some kind of sandstone with bits of darker stone layered and stuck into it. Directly across the lake from it, at the inside corner of the L, was a mound of sticks and mud rising up out of the water a good eight or ten feet. At first Brian couldn't place it but knew that he somehow knew what it was – had seen it in films. Then a small brown head popped to the surface of the water near the mound and began swimming off down the short leg of the L leaving a V of ripples behind and he remembered where he'd seen it. It was a beaver house, called a beaver lodge in a feature film he'd seen on television.

A fish jumped. Not a large fish, but it made a big splash near the beaver, and as if by a signal there were suddenly little plops all over the sides of the lake, along the shore, as fish began jumping. Hundreds of them, jumping and slapping the water. Brian watched them for a time, still in the half-daze, still not thinking well. The scenery was very pretty,

32

he thought, and there were new things to look at, but it was all a green and blue blur and he was used to the grey and black of the city, the sounds of the city. Traffic, people talking, sounds all the time – the hum and whine of the city.

Here, at first, it was silent, or he thought it was silent, but when he started to listen, really listen, he heard thousands of things. Hisses and blurps, small sounds, birds singing, hum of insects, splashes from the fish jumping – there was great noise here, but a noise he did not know, and the colours were new to him, and the colours and noise mixed in his mind to make a green-blue blur that he could hear, hear as a hissing pulse-sound and he was still tired.

So tired.

So awfully tired, and standing had taken a lot of energy somehow, had drained him. He supposed he was still in some kind of shock from the crash and there was still the pain, the dizziness, the strange feeling.

He found another tree, a tall pine with no branches until the top, and sat with his back against it looking down on the lake with the sun warming him, and in a few moments he scrunched down and was asleep again.

FIVE

His eyes snapped open, hammered open, and there were these things about himself that he knew, instantly.

He was unbelievably, viciously thirsty. His mouth was dry and tasted foul and sticky. His lips were cracked and felt as if they were bleeding and if he did not drink some water soon he felt that he would wither up and die. Lots of water. All the water he could find.

He knew the thirst and felt the burn on his face. It was mid-afternoon and the sun had come over him and cooked him while he slept and his face was on fire, would blister, would peel. Which did not help the thirst, made it much worse. He stood, using the tree to pull himself up because there was still some pain and much stiffness, and looked down at the lake.

It was water. But he did not know if he could drink it. Nobody had ever told him if you could or could not drink lakes. There was also the thought of the pilot.

Down in the blue with the plane, strapped in, the body . . .

Awful, he thought. But the lake was blue, and wet-looking, and his mouth and throat raged with the thirst and he did not know where there might be another form of water he could drink. Besides, he

34

had probably swallowed a ton of it while he was swimming out of the plane and getting to shore. In films they always showed the hero finding a clear spring with pure sweet water to drink but in films they didn't have plane wrecks and swollen foreheads and aching bodies and thirst that tore at the hero until he couldn't think.

Brian took small steps down the bank to the lake. Along the edge there were thick grasses and the water looked a little murky and there were small things swimming in the water, small bugs. But there was a log extending about twenty feet out into the water of the lake – a beaver drop from some time before – with old limbs sticking up, almost like handles. He balanced on the log, holding himself up with the limbs, and teetered out past the weeds and murky water.

When he was out where the water was clear and he could see no bugs swimming he kneeled on the log to drink. A sip, he thought, still worrying about the lake water – I'll just take a sip.

But when he brought a cupped hand to his mouth and felt the cold lake water trickle past his cracked lips and over his tongue he could not stop. He had never, not even on long bike trips in the hot summer, been this thirsty. It was as if the water were more than water, as if the water had become all of life, and he could not stop. He stooped and put his mouth to the lake and drank and drank, pulling it deep and swallowing great gulps of it. He drank until his stomach was swollen, until he nearly fell off the log with it, then he rose and stagger-tripped his way back to the bank.

Where he was immediately sick and threw up most

of the water. But his thirst was gone and the water seemed to reduce the pain in his head as well – although the sunburn still cooked his face.

'So.' He almost jumped with the word, spoken aloud. It seemed so out of place, the sound. He tried it again. 'So. So. So here I am.'

And there it is, he thought. For the first time since the crash his mind started to work, his brain triggered and he began thinking.

Here I am – and where is that?

Where am I?

He pulled himself once more up the bank to the tall tree without branches and sat again with his back against the rough bark. It was hot now, but the sun was high and to his rear and he sat in the shade of the tree in relative comfort. There were things to sort out.

Here I am and that is nowhere. With his mind opened and thoughts happening it all tried to come in with a rush, all of what had occurred and he could not take it. The whole thing turned into a confused jumble that made no sense. So he fought it down and tried to take one thing at a time.

He had been flying north to visit his father for a couple of months, in the summer, and the pilot had had a heart attack and had died, and the plane had crashed somewhere in the Canadian north woods but he did not know how far they had flown or in what direction or where he was . . .

Slow down, he thought. Slow down more.

My name is Brian Robeson and I am thirteen years old and I am alone in the north woods of Canada.

All right, he thought, that's simple enough.

I was flying to visit my father and the plane crashed and sank in a lake.

There, keep it that way. Short thoughts.

I do not know where I am.

Which doesn't mean much. More to the point, *they* do not know where I am – *they* meaning anybody who might be wanting to look for me. The searchers.

They would look for him, look for the plane. His father and mother would be frantic. They would tear the world apart to find him. Brian had seen searches on the news, seen films about lost planes. When a plane went down they mounted extensive searches and almost always they found the plane within a day or two. Pilots all filed flight plans – a detailed plan for where and when they were going to fly, with all the courses explained. They would come, they would look for him. The searchers would get government planes and cover both sides of the flight plan filed by the pilot and search until they found him.

Maybe even today. They might come today. This was the second day after the crash. No. Brian frowned. Was it the first day or the second day? They had gone down in the afternoon and he had spent the whole night out cold. So this was the first real day. But they could still come today. They would have started the search immediately when Brian's plane did not arrive.

Yeah, they would probably come today.

Probably come in here with amphibious planes, small bushplanes with floats that could land right here on the lake and pick him up and take him home.

Which home? The father home or the mother home? He stopped the thinking. It didn't matter. Either on to his dad or back to his mother. Either way he would probably be home by late night or early morning, home where he could sit down and eat a large, cheesy, juicy burger with tomatoes and double fries with ketchup and a thick chocolate milkshake.

And there came hunger.

Brian rubbed his stomach. The hunger had been there but something else – fear, pain – had held it down. Now, with the thought of the burger, the emptiness roared at him. He could not believe the hunger, had never felt it this way. The lake water had filled his stomach but left it hungry, and now it demanded food, screamed for food.

And there was, he thought, absolutely nothing to eat.

Nothing.

What did they do in the films when they got stranded like this? Oh, yes, the hero usually found some kind of plant that he knew was good to eat and that took care of it. Just ate the plant until he was full or used some kind of cute trap to catch an animal and cook it over a slick little fire and pretty soon he had a full eight-course meal.

The trouble, Brian thought, looking round, was that all he could see was grass and brush. There was nothing obvious to eat and apart from about a million birds and the beaver he hadn't seen animals to trap and cook, and even if he got one somehow he didn't have any matches so he couldn't have a fire . . .

Nothing.

It kept coming back to that. He had nothing.

Well, almost nothing. As a matter of fact, he thought, I don't know what I've got or haven't got.

Maybe I should try and figure out just how I stand. It will give me something to do – keep me from thinking of food. Until they come to find me.

Brian had once had an English teacher, a guy named Perpich, who was always talking about being positive, thinking positive, staying on top of things. That's how Perpich had put it – stay positive and stay on top of things. Brian thought of him now – wondered how to stay positive and stay on top of this. All Perpich would say is that I have to get motivated. He was always telling kids to get motivated.

Brian changed position so he was sitting on his knees. He reached into his pockets and took out everything he had and laid it on the grass in front of him.

It was pitiful enough. A quarter, three dimes, a nickel, and two pennies. A fingernail clipper. A billfold with a twenty-dollar bill – 'In case you get stranded at the airport in some small town and have to buy food,' his mother had said – and some odd pieces of paper.

And on his belt, somehow still there, the hatchet his mother had given him. He had forgotten it and now reached around and took it out and put it in the grass. There was a touch of rust already forming on the cutting edge of the blade and he rubbed it off with his thumb.

That was it.

He frowned. No, wait – if he was going to play the game, might as well play it right. Perpich would tell him to quit messing around. Get motivated. Look at *all* of it, Robeson.

He had on a pair of good tennis shoes, now almost dry. And socks. And jeans and underwear and a thin leather belt and a T-shirt with an anorak so torn it hung on him in tatters.

And a watch. He had a digital watch still on his wrist but it was broken from the crash – the little screen blank – and he took it off and almost threw it away but stopped the hand motion and lay the watch on the grass with the rest of it.

There. That was it.

No, wait. One other thing. Those were all the things he had, but he also had himself. Perpich used to drum that into them – 'You are your most valuable asset. Don't forget that. *You* are the best thing you have.'

Brian looked around again. I wish you were here, Perpich. I'm hungry and I'd trade everything I have for a hamburger.

'I'm hungry.' He said it aloud. In normal tones at first, then louder and louder until he was yelling it. 'I'm hungry, I'm hungry, I'm hungry!'

When he stopped there was sudden silence, not just from him but the clicks and blurps and bird sounds of the forest as well. The noise of his voice had startled everything and it was quiet. He looked around, listened with his mouth open, and realised that in all his life he had never heard silence before. Complete silence. There had always been some sound, some kind of sound.

It lasted only a few seconds, but it was so intense that it seemed to become part of him. Nothing. There was no sound. Then the bird started again, and some kind of buzzing insect, and then a chattering and a cawing, and soon there was the same background of sound.

Which left him still hungry.

40

Of course, he thought, putting the coins and the rest back in his pocket and the hatchet in his belt – of course if they come tonight or even if they take as long as tomorrow the hunger is no big thing. People have gone for many days without food as long as they've got water. Even if they don't come until late tomorrow I'll be all right. Lose a little weight, maybe, but the first hamburger and a milkshake and fries will bring it right back.

A mental picture of a hamburger, the way they showed it in the television commercials, thundered into his thoughts. Rich colours, the meat juicy and hot . . .

He pushed the picture away. So even if they didn't find him until tomorrow, he thought, he would be all right. He had plenty of water, although he wasn't sure if it was good and clean or not.

He sat again by the tree, his back against it. There was a thing bothering him. He wasn't quite sure what it was but it kept chewing at the edge of his thoughts. Something about the plane and the pilot that would change things . . .

Ah, there it was – the moment when the pilot had his heart attack his right foot had jerked down on the rudder pedal and the plane had slewed sideways. What did that mean? Why did that keep coming into his thinking that way, nudging and pushing?

It means, a voice in his thoughts said, that they might not be coming for you tonight or even tomorrow. When the pilot pushed the rudder pedal the plane had jerked to the side and assumed a new course. Brian could not remember how much it had pulled round, but it wouldn't have had to be much

41

because after that, with the pilot dead, Brian had flown for hour after hour on the new course.

Well away from the flight plan the pilot had filed. Many hours, at maybe 160 miles an hour. Even if it was only a little off course, with that speed and time Brian might now be sitting several hundred miles off to the side of the recorded flight plan.

And they would probably search most heavily at first along the flight plan course. They might go out to the side a little, but he could easily be three, four hundred miles to the side. He could not know, could not think of how far he might have flown wrong because he didn't know the original course and didn't know how much they had pulled sideways.

Quite a bit – that's how he remembered it. Quite a jerk to the side. It pulled his head over sharply when the plane had swung around.

They might not find him for two or three days. He felt his heartbeat increase as the fear started. The thought was there but he fought it down for a time, pushed it away, then it exploded out.

They might not find him for a long time.

And the next thought was there as well, that they might never find him, but that was panic and he fought it down and tried to stay positive. They searched hard when a plane went down, they used many men and planes and they would go to the side, they would know he was off from the flight path, he had talked to the man on the radio, they would somehow know . . .

It would be all right.

They would find him. Maybe not tomorrow, but soon. Soon. Soon.

They would find him soon.

Gradually, like sloshing oil his thoughts settled back and the panic was gone. Say they didn't come for two days – no, say they didn't come for three days, even push that to four days – he could live with that. He would have to live with that. He didn't want to think of them taking longer. But say four days. He had to do something. He couldn't just sit at the bottom of this tree and stare down at the lake for four days.

And nights. He was in deep woods and didn't have any matches, couldn't make a fire. There were large things in the woods. There were wolves, he thought, and bears – other things. In the dark he would be in the open here, just sitting at the bottom of a tree.

He looked around suddenly, felt the hair on the back of his neck go up. Things might be looking at him right now, waiting for him – waiting for dark so they could move in and take him.

He fingered the hatchet at his belt. It was the only weapon he had, but it was something.

He had to have some kind of shelter. No, make that more: he had to have some kind of shelter and he had to have something to eat.

He pulled himself to his feet and jerked the back of his shirt down before the mosquitoes could get at it. He had to do something to help himself.

I have to get motivated, he thought, remembering Perpich. Right now I'm all I've got. I have to do something.

43

SIX

Two years before he and Terry had been fooling around down near the park, where the city seemed to end for a time and the trees grew thick and came down to the small river that went through the park. It was thick there and seemed kind of wild, and they had been joking and making things up and they pretended that they were lost in the woods and talked in the afternoon about what they would do. Of course they figured they'd have all sorts of goodies like a gun and a knife and fishing gear and matches so they could hunt and fish and have a fire.

I wish you were here, Terry, he thought. With a gun and a knife and some matches . . .

In the park that time they had decided the best shelter was a lean-to and Brian set out now to make one up. Maybe cover it with grass or leaves or sticks, he thought, and he started to go down to the lake again, where there were some willows he could cut down for supports. But it struck him that he ought to find a good place for the lean-to and so he decided to look around first. He wanted to stay near the lake because he thought the plane, even deep in the water, might show up to somebody flying over and he didn't want to diminish any chance he might have of being found.

His eyes fell upon the stone ridge to his left and he thought at first he should build his shelter against the stone. But before that he decided to check out the far side of the ridge and that was where he got lucky.

Using the sun and the fact that it rose in the east and set in the west, he decided that the far side was the northern side of the ridge. At one time in the far past it had been scooped by something, probably a glacier, and this scooping had left a kind of sideways bowl, back in under a ledge. It wasn't very deep, not a cave, but it was smooth and made a perfect roof and he could almost stand in under the ledge. He had to hold his head slightly tipped forward at the front to keep it from hitting the top. Some of the rock that had been scooped out had also been pulverised by the glacial action turned into sand, and now made a small sand beach that went down to the edge of the water in front and to the right of the overhang.

It was his first good luck.

No, he thought. He had good luck in the landing. But this was good luck as well, luck he needed.

All he had to do was wall off part of the bowl and leave an opening as a doorway and he would have a perfect shelter – much stronger than a lean-to and dry because the overhang made a watertight roof.

He crawled back in, under the ledge, and sat. The sand was cool here in the shade, and the coolness felt wonderful to his face, which was already starting to blister and get especially painful on his forehead, with the blisters on top of the swelling.

He was also still weak. Just the walk around the back of the ridge and the slight climb over the top had left his legs rubbery. It felt good to sit for a bit under the shade of the overhang in the cool sand.

And now, he thought, if I just had something to eat.

45

Anything.

When he had rested a bit he went back down to the lake and drank a couple of swallows of water. He wasn't all that thirsty but he thought the water might help to take the edge off his hunger. It didn't. Somehow the cold lake water actually made it worse, sharpened it.

He thought of dragging in wood to make a wall on part of the overhang, and picked up one piece to pull up, but his arms were too weak and he knew then that it wasn't just the crash and injury to his body and head, it was also that he was weak from hunger.

He would have to find something to eat. Before he did anything else he would have to have something to eat.

But what?

Brian leaned against the rock and stared out at the lake. What, in all of this, was there to eat? He was so used to having food just be there, just always being there. When he was hungry he went to the fridge, or to the shops, or sat down at a meal his mother cooked.

Oh, he thought, remembering a meal now – oh. It was the last Thanksgiving, last year, the last Thanksgiving they had as a family before his mother demanded the divorce and his father moved out in the following January. Brian already knew the Secret but did not know it would cause them to break up and thought it might work out, the Secret that his father still did not know but that he would try to tell him. When he saw him.

The meal had been turkey and they cooked it in the back yard in the barbecue over charcoal with the lid down tight. His father had put chips of hickory wood on the charcoal and the smell of the cooking turkey and the hickory smoke had filled the yard. When his father took the lid off, smiling, the smell that had come out was unbelievable, and when they sat to eat the meat was wet with juice and rich and had the taste of the smoke in it . . .

He had to stop this. His mouth was full of saliva and his stomach was twisting and growling.

What was there to eat?

What had he read or seen that told him about food in the wilderness? Hadn't there been something? A programme, yes, a programme on television about air force pilots and some kind of course they took. A survival course. All right, he had the programme coming into his thoughts now. The pilots had to live in the desert. They put them in the desert down in Arizona or someplace and they had to live for a week. They had to find food and water for a week.

For water they had made a sheet of plastic into a dew-gathering device and for food they ate lizards.

That was it. Of course Brian had lots of water and there weren't too many lizards in the Canadian woods, that he knew. One of the pilots had used a watch crystal as a magnifying glass to focus the sun and start a fire so they didn't have to eat the lizards raw. But Brian had a digital watch, without a crystal, broken at that. So the programme didn't help him much.

Wait, there was one thing. One of the pilots, a woman, had found some kind of beans on a bush and she had used them with her lizard meat to make a little stew in a tin can she had found. Bean lizard stew. There weren't any beans here, but there must be berries. There had to be berry bushes around. Sure, the woods were full of berry bushes. That's what everybody always said. Well, he'd actually never heard anybody *say* it. But he felt that it should be true.

There must be berry bushes.

He stood and moved out into the sand and looked up at the sun. It was still high. He didn't know what time it must be. At home it would be one or two if the sun were that high. At home at one or two his mother would be putting away the lunch dishes and getting ready for her exercise class. No, that would have been yesterday. Today she would be going to see *him*. Today was Thursday and she always went to see him on Thursdays. Wednesday was the exercise class and Thursday she went to see him. Hot little jets of hate worked into his thoughts, pushed once, moved back. If his mother hadn't begun to see *him* and forced the divorce, Brian wouldn't be here now.

He shook his head. Had to stop that kind of thinking. The sun was still high and that meant that he had some time before darkness to find berries. He didn't want to be away from his – he almost thought of it as home – shelter when it came to be dark.

He didn't want to be anywhere in the woods when it came to be dark. And he didn't want to get lost – which was a real problem. All he knew in the world was the lake in front of him and the hill at his back and the ridge – if he lost sight of them there was a really good chance that he would get turned round and not find his way back.

So he had to look for berry bushes, but keep the lake or the rock ridge in sight at all times.

He looked up the lake shore, to the north. For a

good distance, perhaps two hundred yards, it was fairly clear. There were tall pines, the kind with no limbs until very close to the top, with a gentle breeze sighing in them, but not too much low brush. Two hundred yards up there seemed to be a belt of thick, lower brush starting – about ten or twelve feet high – and that formed a wall he could not see through. It seemed to go on around the lake, thick and lushly green, but he could not be sure.

If there were berries they would be in that brush, he felt, and as long as he stayed close to the lake, so he could keep the water on his right and know it was there, he wouldn't get lost. When he was done or found berries, he thought, he would just turn round so the water was on his left and walk back until he came to the ridge and his shelter.

Simple. Keep it simple. I am Brian Robeson. I have been in a plane crash. I am going to find some food. I am going to find berries.

He walked slowly – still a bit pained in his joints and weak from hunger – up along the side of the lake. The trees were full of birds singing ahead of him in the sun. Some he knew, some he didn't. He saw a robin, and some kind of sparrows, and a flock of reddish orange birds with thick beaks. Twenty or thirty of them were sitting in one of the pines. They made much noise and flew away ahead of him when he walked under the tree. He watched them fly, their colour a bright slash in solid green, and in this way he found the berries. The birds landed in some taller willow type of undergrowth with wide leaves and started jumping and making noise. At first he was too far away to see what they were doing, but their colour drew him and he moved towards them, keeping the lake in sight on his right, and when he got closer he saw they were eating berries.

He could not believe it was that easy. It was as if the birds had taken him right to the berries. The slender branches went up about twenty feet and were heavy, drooping with clusters of bright red berries. They were half as big as grapes but hung in bunches much like grapes and when Brian saw them, glistening red in the sunlight, he almost yelled.

His pace quickened and he was in them in moments, scattering the birds, grabbing branches, stripping them to fill his mouth with berries.

He almost spat them out. It wasn't that they were bitter so much as that they lacked any sweetness, had a tart flavour that left his mouth dry feeling. And they were like cherries in that they had large pips, which made them hard to chew. But there was such a hunger on him, such an emptiness, that he could not stop and kept stripping branches and eating berries by the handful, grabbing and jamming them into his mouth and swallowing them pips and all.

He could not stop and when, at last, his stomach was full he was still hungry. Two days without food must have shrunk his stomach, but the drive of hunger was still there. Thinking of the birds, and how they would come back into the berries when he left, he made a carrying pouch of his torn anorak and kept picking. Finally, when he judged he had close to four pounds in the jacket he stopped and went back to his camp by the ridge.

Now, he thought. Now I have some food and I can do something about fixing this place up. He glanced at the sun and saw he had some time before dark.

If only I had matches, he thought, looking ruefully

at the beach and lakeside. There was driftwood every-where, not to mention dead and dry wood all over the hill and dead-dry branches hanging from every tree. All firewood. And no matches. How used they to do it, he thought. Rub two sticks together?

He tucked the berries in the pouch back in under the overhang in the cool shade and found a couple of sticks. After ten minutes of rubbing he felt the sticks and they were almost cool to the touch. Not that, he thought. They didn't do fire that way. He threw the sticks down in disgust. So no fire. But he could still fix the shelter and make it – here the word 'safer' came into his mind and he didn't know why – more livable.

Kind of close it in, he thought. I'll just close it in a bit.

He started dragging sticks up from the lake and pulling long dead branches down from the hill, never getting out of sight of the water and the ridge. With these he interlaced and wove a wall across the opening of the front of the rock. It took over two hours, and he had to stop several times because he still felt a bit weak and once because he felt a strange new twinge in his stomach. A tightening, rolling. Too many berries, he thought. I ate too many of them.

But it was gone soon and he kept working until the entire front of the overhang was covered save for a small opening at the right end, nearest the lake. The doorway was about three feet, and when he went in he found himself in a room almost fifteen feet long and eight to ten feet deep, with the rock wall sloping down at the rear.

'Good,' he said, nodding. 'Good . . .'

Outside the sun was going down, finally, and in

the initial coolness the mosquitoes came out again and clouded in on him. They were thick, terrible, if not quite as bad as in the morning, and he kept brushing them off his arms until he couldn't stand it and then dumped the berries and put the torn anorak on. At least the sleeves covered his arms.

Wrapped in the jacket, with darkness coming down fast now, he crawled back in under the rock and huddled and tried to sleep. He was deeply tired, and still aching a bit, but sleep was slow coming and did not finally settle in until the evening cool turned to night cool and the mosquitoes slowed.

Then, at last, with his stomach turning on the berries, Brian went to sleep.

SEVEN

'Mother!'

He screamed it and he could not be sure if the scream awakened him or the pain in his stomach. His whole abdomen was torn with great rolling jolts of pain, pain that doubled him in the darkness of the little shelter, put him over and face down in the sand to moan again and again: 'Mother, mother, mother . . .'

Never anything like this. Never. It was as if all the berries, all the pips had exploded in the centre of him, ripped and tore at him. He crawled out of the doorway and was sick in the sand, then crawled still further and was sick again, vomiting and with terrible diarrhoea for over an hour, for over a year he thought, until he was at last empty and drained of all strength.

Then he crawled back into the shelter and fell again to the sand but could not sleep at first, could do nothing except lie there, and his mind decided then to bring the memory up again.

In the mall. Every detail. His mother sitting in the car with the man. And she had leaned across and kissed him, kissed the man with the short blond hair, and it was not a friendly peck, but a kiss. A kiss where she turned her head over at an angle and put her mouth against the mouth of the blond man who was not his father and kissed, mouth to mouth, and then brought her hand up to touch his cheek, his forehead, while they were kissing. And Brian saw it.

Saw this thing that his mother did with the blond man. Saw the kiss that became the Secret that his father still did not know about, know all about.

The memory was so real that he could feel the heat in the mall that day, could remember the worry that Terry would turn and see his mother, could remember the worry of the shame of it and then the memory faded and he slept again . . .

Awake.

For a second, perhaps two, he did not know where he was, was still in his sleep somewhere. Then he saw the sun streaming in the open doorway of the shelter and heard the close, vicious whine of the mosquitoes and knew. He brushed his face, completely welted now with two days of bites, completely covered with lumps and bites, and was surprised to find the swelling on his forehead had gone down a great deal, was almost gone.

The smell was awful and he couldn't place it. Then he saw the pile of berries at the back of the shelter and remembered the night and being sick.

'Too many of them,' he said aloud. 'Too many gut cherries . . .'

He crawled out of the shelter and found where he'd messed the sand. He used sticks and cleaned it as best he could, covered it with clean sand and went down to the lake to wash his hands and get a drink.

It was still very early, only just past true dawn, and the water was so calm he could see his reflection. It frightened him – the face was cut and bleeding, swollen and lumpy, the hair all matted, and on his forehead a cut had healed but left the hair stuck with blood and scab. His eyes were slits in the bites and he was – somehow – covered with dirt. He slapped the water with his hand to destroy the mirror.

Ugly, he thought. Very, very ugly.

And he was, at that moment, almost overcome with self-pity. He was dirty and starving and bitten and hurt and lonely and ugly and afraid and so completely miserable that it was like being in a pit, a dark, deep pit with no way out.

He sat back on the bank and fought crying. Then let it come and cried for perhaps three, four minutes. Long tears, self-pity tears, wasted tears.

He stood, went back to the water, and took small drinks. As soon as the cold water hit his stomach he felt the hunger sharpen, as it had before, and he stood and held his abdomen until the hunger cramps receded.

He had to eat. He was weak with it again, down with the hunger, and he had to eat.

Back at the shelter the berries lay in a pile where he had dumped them when he grabbed his anorak – gut cherries he called them in his mind now – and he thought of eating some of them. Not such a crazy amount, as he had, which he felt brought on the sickness in the night – but just enough to stave off the hunger a bit.

He crawled into the shelter. Some flies were on the berries and he brushed them off. He selected only the berries that were solidly ripe – not the light red ones, but the berries that were dark, maroon red to black and swollen in ripeness. When he had a small handful of them he went back down to the lake and washed them in the water – small fish scattered away when he splashed the water up and he wished he had a fishing line and hook – then he ate them carefully, spitting out the pips. They were still tart, but had a sweetness to them, although they seemed to make his lips a bit numb.

When he finished he was still hungry, but the edge was gone and his legs didn't feel as weak as they had.

He went back to the shelter. It took him half an hour to go through the rest of the berries and sort them, putting all the fully ripe ones in a pile on some leaves, the rest in another pile. When he was done he covered the two piles with grass he tore from the lake shore to keep the flies off and went back outside.

They were awful berries, those gut cherries, he thought. But there was food there, food of some kind, and he could eat a bit more later tonight if he had to.

For now he had a full day ahead of him. He looked at the sky through the trees and saw that while there were clouds they were scattered and did not seem to hold rain. There was a light breeze that seemed to keep the mosquitoes down and, he thought, looking up along the lake shore, if there was one kind of berry there should be other kinds. Sweeter kinds.

If he kept the lake in sight as he had done yesterday he should be all right, should be able to find home again – and it stopped him. He had actually thought it that time.

Home. Three days, no, two – or was it three? Yes, this was the third day and he had thought of the shelter as home.

He turned and looked at it, studied the crude work. The brush made a fair wall, not weathertight but it cut most of the wind off. He hadn't done so badly at that. Maybe it wasn't much, but also maybe it was all he had for a home.

All right, he thought, so I'll call it home.

He turned back and set off up the side of the lake, heading for the gut cherry bushes, his anorak bag in his hand. Things were bad, he thought, but maybe not that bad.

Maybe he could find some better berries.

When he came to the gut cherry bushes he paused. The branches were empty of birds but still had many berries, and some of those that had been merely red yesterday were now a dark maroon to black. Much riper. Maybe he should stay and pick them to save them.

But the explosion in the night was still much in his memory and he decided to go on. Gut cherries were food, but tricky to eat. He needed something better.

Another hundred yards up the shore there was a place where the wind had torn another path. These must have been fierce winds, he thought, to tear places up like this – as they had the path he had found with the plane when he crashed. Here the trees were not all the way down but twisted and snapped off halfway up from the ground, so their tops were all down and rotted and gone, leaving the snags poking into the sky like broken teeth. It made for tons of dead and dry wood and he wished once more he could get a fire going. It also made a kind of clearing – with the tops of the trees gone the sun could get down to the ground – and it was filled with small thorny bushes that were covered with berries.

Raspberries.

These he knew because there were some raspberry

bushes in the park and he and Terry were always picking and eating them when they biked past.

The berries were full and ripe, and he tasted one to find it sweet, and with none of the problems of the gut cherries. Although they did not grow in clusters, there were many of them and they were easy to pick and Brian smiled and started eating.

Sweet juice, he thought. Oh, they were sweet with just a tiny tang and he picked and ate and picked and ate and thought that he had never tasted anything this good. Soon, as before, his stomach was full, but now he had some sense and he did not gorge or cram more down. Instead he picked more and put them in his anorak, feeling the morning sun on his back and thinking he was rich, rich with food now, just rich, and he heard a noise to his rear, a slight noise, and he turned and saw the bear.

He could do nothing, think nothing. His tongue, stained with berry juice, stuck to the roof of his mouth and he stared at the bear. It was black, with a cinnamon-coloured nose, not twenty feet from him and big. No, huge. It was all black fur and huge. He had seen one in the zoo in the city once, a black bear, but it had been from India or somewhere. This one was wild, and much bigger than the one in the zoo and it was right there.

Right there.

The sun caught the ends of the hairs along its back. Shining black and silky the bear stood on its hind legs, half up, and studied Brian, just studied him, then lowered itself and moved slowly to the left, eating berries as it rolled along, wuffling and delicately using its mouth to lift each berry from the stem, and in seconds it was gone. Gone, and Brian still had not moved. His tongue was stuck to the top of his mouth, the tip half out, his eyes were wide and his hands were reaching for a berry.

Then he made a sound, a low: 'Nnnnnnggg.' It made no sense, was just a sound of fear, of disbelief that something that large could have come so close to him without his knowing. It just walked up to him and could have eaten him and he could have done nothing. Nothing. And when the sound was half done a thing happened with his legs, a thing he had nothing to do with, and they were running in the opposite direction from the bear, back towards the shelter.

He would have run all the way, in panic, but after he had gone perhaps fifty yards his brain took over and slowed and, finally, stopped him.

If the bear had wanted you, his brain said, he would have taken you. It is something to understand, he thought, not something to run away from. The bear was eating berries.

Not people.

The bear made no move to hurt you, to threaten you. It stood to see you better, study you, then went on its way eating berries. It was a big bear, but it did not want you, did not want to cause you harm, and that is the thing to understand here.

He turned and looked back at the stand of raspberries. The bear was gone, the birds were singing, he saw nothing that could hurt him. There was no danger here that he could sense, could feel. In the city, at night, there was sometimes danger. You could not be in the park at night, after dark, because of the danger. But here, the bear had looked at him and had

59

moved on and – this filled his thoughts – the berries were so good.

So good. So sweet and rich and his body was so empty.

And the bear had almost indicated that it didn't mind sharing – had just walked from him.

And the berries were so good.

And he thought, finally, if he did not go back and get the berries he would have to eat the gut cherries again tonight.

That convinced him and he walked slowly back to the raspberry patch and continued picking for the entire morning, although with great caution, and once when a squirrel rustled some pine needles at the base of a tree he nearly jumped out of his skin.

About noon – the sun was almost straight overhead – the clouds began to thicken and look dark. In moments it started to rain and he took what he had picked and trotted back to the shelter. He had eaten probably two pounds of raspberries and had maybe another three pounds in his jacket, rolled in a pouch.

He made it to the shelter just as the clouds completely opened and the rain roared down in sheets. Soon the sand outside was drenched and there were rivulets running down to the lake. But inside he was dry and snug. He started to put the picked berries back in the sorted pile with the gut cherries but noticed that the raspberries were seeping through the jacket. They were much softer than the gut cherries and apparently were being crushed a bit with their own weight.

When he held the jacket up and looked beneath it he saw a stream of red liquid. He put a finger in it and found it to be sweet and tangy, like pop without the fizz, and he grinned and lay back on the sand, holding the bag up over his face and letting the seepage drip into his mouth.

Outside the rain poured down, but Brian lay back, drinking the syrup from the berries, dry and with the pain almost gone, the stiffness also gone, his belly full and a good taste in his mouth.

For the first time since the crash he was not thinking of himself, of his own life. Brian was wondering if the bear was as surprised as he to find another being in the berries.

Later in the afternoon, as evening came down, he went to the lake and washed the sticky berry juice from his face and hands, then went back to prepare for the night.

While he had accepted and understood that the bear did not want to hurt him, it was still much in his thoughts and as darkness came into the shelter he took the hatchet out of his belt and put it by his head, his hand on the handle, as the day caught up with him and he slept.

EIGHT

At first he thought it was a growl. In the still darkness of the shelter in the middle of the night his eyes came open and he was awake and he thought there was a growl. But it was the wind, a medium wind in the pines had made some sound and brought him up, brought him awake. He sat up and was hit with the smell.

It terrified him. The smell was one of rot, some musty rot that made him think only of graves with cobwebs and dust and old death. His nostrils widened and he opened his eyes wider but he could see nothing. It was too dark, too hard dark with clouds covering even the small light from the stars, and he could not see. But the smell was alive, alive and full and in the shelter. He thought of the bear, thought of Bigfoot and every monster he had ever seen in every horror film he had ever watched, and his heart hammered in his throat.

Then he heard the slithering. A brushing sound, a slithering brushing sound near his feet — and he kicked out as hard as he could, kicked out and threw the hatchet at the sound, a noise coming from his throat. But the hatchet missed, sailed into the wall where it hit the rocks with a shower of sparks, and his leg was instantly torn with pain, as if a hundred needles had been driven into it. 'Unnnngh!'

Now he screamed, with the pain and fear, and

skittered on his backside up into the corner of the shelter, breathing through his mouth, straining to see, to hear.

The slithering moved again, he thought towards him at first, and terror took him, stopping his breath. He felt he could see a low dark form, a bulk in the darkness, a shadow that lived, but now it moved away, slithering and scraping it moved away and he saw or thought he saw it go out of the door opening.

He lay on his side for a moment, then pulled a rasping breath in and held it, listening for the attacker to return. When it was apparent that the shadow wasn't coming back he felt the calf of his leg, where the pain was centred, and spreading to fill the whole leg.

His fingers gingerly touched a group of needles that had been driven through his trousers and into the fleshy part of his calf. They were stiff and very sharp on the ends that stuck out, and he knew then what the attacker had been. A porcupine had stumbled into his shelter and when he had kicked it the thing had slapped him with its tail of quills.

He touched each quill carefully. The pain made it seem as if dozens of them had been slammed into his leg, but there were only eight, pinning the cloth against his skin. He leaned back against the wall for a minute. He couldn't leave them in, they had to come out, but just touching them made the pain more intense.

So fast, he thought. So fast things change. When he'd gone to sleep he had satisfaction and in just a moment it was all different. He grasped one of the quills, held his breath, and jerked. It sent pain signals to his brain in tight waves, but he grabbed another, pulled it, then another quill. When he had pulled four of them he stopped for a moment. The pain had gone from being a pointed injury pain to spreading in a hot smear up his leg and it made him catch his breath.

Some of the quills were driven in deeper than others and they tore when they came out. He breathed deeply twice, let half of the breath out, and went back to work. Jerk, pause, jerk – and three more times before he lay back in the darkness, done. The pain filled his leg now, and with it came new waves of self-pity. Sitting alone in the dark, his leg aching, some mosquitoes finding him again, he started crying. It was all too much, just too much, and he couldn't take it. Not the way it was.

I can't take it this way, alone with no fire and in the dark, and next time it might be something worse, maybe a bear, and it wouldn't be just quills in the leg, it would be worse. I can't do this, he thought, again and again. I can't. Brian pulled himself up until he was sitting upright back in the corner of the cave. He put his head down on his arms across his knees, with stiffness taking his left leg, and cried until he was cried out.

He did not know how long it took, but later he looked back on this time of crying in the corner of the dark cave and thought of it as when he learned the most important rule of survival, which was that feeling sorry for yourself didn't work. It wasn't just that it was wrong to do, or that it was considered incorrect. It was more than that – it didn't work. When he sat alone in the darkness and cried and was done, was all done with it, nothing had changed. His leg still hurt, it was still dark, he was still alone and the self-pity had accomplished nothing.

At last he slept again, but already his patterns were changing and the sleep was light, a resting doze more than a deep sleep, with small sounds awakening him twice in the rest of the night. In the last doze period before daylight, before he awakened finally with the morning light and the clouds of new mosquitoes, he dreamed. This time it was not of his mother, not of the Secret, but of his father at first and then of his friend Terry.

In the initial segment of the dream his father was standing at the side of a living room looking at him and it was clear from his expression that he was trying to tell Brian something. His lips moved but there was no sound, not a whisper. He waved his hands at Brian, made gestures in front of his face as if he were scratching something, and he worked to make a word with his mouth but at first Brian could not see it. Then the lips made an *mmmmm* shape but no sound came. *Mmmmm-maaaa.* Brian could not hear it, could not understand it and he wanted to so badly; it was so important to understand his father, to know what he was saying. He was trying to help, trying so hard, and when Brian couldn't understand he looked cross, the way he did when Brian asked questions more than once, and he faded. Brian's father faded into a fog place Brian could not see and the dream was almost over, or seemed to be, when Terry came.

He was not gesturing to Brian but was sitting in the park on a bench looking at a barbecue pit and for a time nothing happened. Then he got up and poured some charcoal from a bag into the cooker, then some starter fluid, and he took a flick type of lighter and lit the fluid. When it was burning and the charcoal was at last getting hot he turned, noticing Brian for the first time in the dream. He turned and smiled and pointed to the fire as if to say, see, a fire.

But it meant nothing to Brian, except that he wished he had a fire. He saw a grocery bag on the table next to Terry. Brian thought it must contain hot dogs and chips and mustard and he could think only of the food. But Terry shook his head and pointed again to the fire, and twice more he pointed to the fire, made Brian see the flames, and Brian felt his frustration and anger rise and he thought all right, all right, I see the fire but so what? I don't have a fire. I know about fire; I know I need a fire.

I know that.

His eyes opened and there was light in the cave, a grey dim light of morning. He wiped his mouth and tried to move his leg, which had stiffened like wood. There was thirst, and hunger, and he ate some rasp-berries from the jacket. They had spoiled a bit, seemed softer and mushier, but still had a rich sweet-ness. He crushed the berries against the roof of his mouth with his tongue and drank the sweet juice as it ran down his throat. A flash of metal caught his eye and he saw his hatchet in the sand where he had thrown it at the porcupine in the dark.

He scootched up, wincing a bit when he bent his stiff leg, and crawled to where the hatchet lay. He picked it up and examined it and saw a chip in the top of the head.

The nick wasn't large, but the hatchet was important to him, was his only tool, and he should not have thrown it. He should keep it in his hand, and make a tool of some kind to help push an animal away. Make a staff, he thought, or a lance, and save the hatchet. Something came then, a thought as he held the hatchet, something about the dream and his father and Terry, but he couldn't pin it down.

'Ahhh . . .' He scrambled out and stood in the morning sun and stretched his back muscles and his sore leg. The hatchet was still in his hand, and as he stretched and raised it over his head it caught the first rays of the morning sun. The first faint light hit the silver of the hatchet and it flashed a brilliant gold in the light. Like fire. That is it, he thought. What they were trying to tell me.

Fire. The hatchet was the key to it all. When he threw the hatchet at the porcupine in the cave and missed and hit the stone wall it had showered sparks, a golden shower of sparks in the dark, as golden with fire as the sun was now.

The hatchet was the answer. That's what his father and Terry had been trying to tell him. Somehow he could get fire from the hatchet. The sparks would make fire.

Brian went back into the shelter and studied the wall. It was some form of chalky granite, or a sandstone, but imbedded in it were large pieces of a darker stone, a harder and darker stone. It only took him a moment to find where the hatchet had struck. The steel had nicked into the edge of one of the darker stone pieces. Brian turned the head backward so he would strike with the flat rear of the hatchet and hit the black rock gently. Too gently, and nothing happened. He struck harder, a glancing blow, and two or three weak sparks skipped off the rock and died immediately.

He swung harder, held the hatchet so it would hit a longer, sliding blow, and the black rock exploded in fire. Sparks flew so heavily that several of them skittered and jumped on the sand beneath the rock and he smiled and struck again and again.

There could be fire here, he thought. I will have a fire here, he thought, and struck again – I will have fire from the hatchet.

NINE

Brian found it was a long way from sparks to fire.

Clearly there had to be something for the sparks to ignite, some kind of tinder or kindling – but what? He brought some dried grass in, tapped sparks into it and watched them die. He tried small twigs, breaking them into little pieces, but that was worse than the grass. Then he tried a combination of the two, grass and twigs.

Nothing. He had no trouble getting sparks, but the tiny bits of hot stone or metal – he couldn't tell which they were – just sputtered and died.

He settled back on his haunches in exasperation, looking at the pitiful clump of grass and twigs.

He needed something finer, something soft and fine and fluffy to catch the bits of fire.

Shredded paper would be nice, but he had no paper.

'So close,' he said aloud, 'so close . . .'

He put the hatchet back in his belt and went out of the shelter, limping on his sore leg. There had to be something, had to be. Man had made fire. There had been fire for thousands, millions of years. There had to be a way. He dug in his pockets and found the twenty-dollar bill in his wallet. Paper. Worthless paper out here. But if he could get a fire going . . .

He ripped the twenty into tiny pieces, made a pile

of pieces, and hit sparks into them. Nothing happened. They just wouldn't take the sparks. But there had to be a way – some way to do it.

Not twenty feet to his right, leaning out over the water, were birches and he stood looking at them for a full half-minute before they registered on his mind. They were a beautiful white with bark like clean, slightly speckled paper.

Paper.

He moved to the trees. Where the bark was peeling from the trunks it lifted in tiny tendrils, almost fluffs. Brian plucked some of them loose, rolled them in his fingers. They seemed flammable, dry and nearly powdery. He pulled and twisted bits off the trees, packing them in one hand while he picked them with the other, picking and gathering until he had a wad close to the size of a baseball.

Then he went back into the shelter and arranged the ball of birchbark peelings at the base of the black rock. As an afterthought he threw in the remains of the twenty-dollar bill. He struck and a stream of sparks fell into the bark and quickly died. But this time one spark fell on one small hair of dry bark – almost a thread of bark – and seemed to glow a bit brighter before it died.

The material had to be finer. There had to be a soft and incredibly fine nest for the sparks.

I must make a home for the sparks, he thought. A perfect home or they won't stay, they won't make fire.

He started ripping the bark, using his fingernails at first, and when that didn't work he used the sharp edge of the hatchet, cutting the bark in thin slivers, hairs so fine they were almost not there. It was painstaking work, slow work, and he stayed with it for over two hours. Twice he stopped for a handful of berries and once to go to the lake for a drink. Then back to work, the sun on his back, until at last he had a ball of fluff as big as a grapefruit – dry birch-bark fluff.

He positioned his spark nest – as he thought of it – at the base of the rock, used his thumb to make a small depression in the middle, and slammed the back of the hatchet down across the black rock. A cloud of sparks rained down, most of them missing the nest, but some, perhaps thirty or so, hit in the depression and of those six or seven found fuel and grew, smouldered and caused the bark to take on the red glow.

Then they went out.

Close – he was close. He repositioned the nest, made a new and smaller dent with his thumb, and struck again.

More sparks, a slight glow, then nothing.

It's me, he thought. I'm doing something wrong. I do not know this – a cave dweller would have had a fire by now, a Cro-Magnon man would have a fire by now – but I don't know this. I don't know how to make a fire.

Maybe not enough sparks. He settled the nest in place once more and hit the rock with a series of blows, as fast as he could. The sparks poured like a golden waterfall. At first they seemed to take, there were several, many sparks that found life and took briefly, but they all died.

Starved.

He leaned back. They are like me. They are starving. It wasn't quantity, there were plenty of sparks, but they needed more.

71

I would kill, he thought suddenly, for a box of matches. Just one box. Just one match. I would kill.

What makes fire? He thought back to school. To all those science classes. Had he ever learned what made a fire? Did a teacher ever stand up there and say, 'This is what makes a fire . . .'

He shook his head, tried to focus his thoughts. What did it take? You have to have fuel, he thought – and he had that. The bark was fuel. Oxygen – there had to be air.

He needed to add air. He had to fan on it, blow on it.

He made the nest ready again, held the hatchet back, tensed, and struck four quick blows. Sparks came down and he leaned forward as fast as be could and blew.

Too hard. There was a bright, almost intense glow, then it was gone. He had blown it out.

Another set of strikes, more sparks. He leaned and blew, but gently this time, holding back and aiming the stream of air from his mouth to hit the brightest spot. Five or six sparks had fallen in a tight mass of bark hair and Brian centred his efforts there.

The sparks grew with his gentle breath. The red glow moved from the sparks themselves into the bark, moved and grew and became worms, glowing red worms that crawled up the bark hairs and caught other threads of bark and grew until there was a pocket of red as big as a quarter, a glowing red coal of heat.

And when he ran out of breath and paused to inhale, the red ball suddenly burst into flame.

'Fire!' he yelled. 'I've got fire! I've got it, I've got it, I've got it . . .'

But the flames were thick and oily and burning fast, consuming the ball of bark as fast as if it were petrol. He had to feed the flames, keep them going. Working as fast as he could he carefully placed the dried grass and wood pieces he had tried at first on top of the bark and was gratified to see them take.

But they would go fast. He needed more, and more. He could not let the flames go out.

He ran from the shelter to the pines and started breaking off the low, dead small limbs. These he threw in the shelter, went back for more, threw those in, and squatted to break and feed the hungry flames. When the small wood was going well he went out and found larger wood and did not relax until that was going. Then he leaned back against the wood brace of his door opening and smiled.

I have a friend, he thought – I have a friend now. A hungry friend, but a good one. I have a friend named fire.

'Hello, fire . . .'

The curve of the rock back made an almost perfect drawing flue that carried the smoke up through the cracks of the roof but held the heat. If he kept the fire small it would be perfect and would keep anything like the porcupine from coming through the door again.

A friend and a guard, he thought.

So much from a little spark. A friend and a guard from a tiny spark.

He looked around and wished he had somebody to tell this thing, to show this thing he had done. But there was nobody.

Nothing but the trees and the sun and the breeze and the lake.

Nobody.

And he thought, rolling thoughts, with the smoke curling up over his head and the smile still half on his face he thought: I wonder what they're doing now.

I wonder what my father is doing now.

I wonder what my mother is doing now.

I wonder if she is with him.

TEN

He could not at first leave the fire.

It was so precious to him, so close and sweet a
thing, the yellow and red flames brightening the dark
interior of the shelter, the happy crackle of the dry
wood as it burned, that he could not leave it. He
went to the trees and brought in as many dead limbs
as he could chop off and carry, and when he had a
large pile of them he sat near the fire – though it was
getting into the warm middle part of the day and he
was hot – and broke them in small pieces and fed the
fire.

I will not let you go out, he said to himself to the
flames – not ever. And so he sat through a long part
of the day, keeping the flames even, eating from his
stock of raspberries, leaving to drink from the lake
when he was thirsty. In the afternoon, towards
evening, with his face smoke-smeared and his skin
red from the heat, he finally began to think ahead to
what he needed to do.

He would need a large woodpile to get through
the night. It would be almost impossible to find wood
in the dark so he had to have it all in and cut and
stacked before the sun went down.

Brian made certain the fire was banked with new
wood, then went out of the shelter and searched for
a good fuel supply. Up the hill from the campsite
the same windstorm that left him a place to land the

75

plane – had that only been three, four days ago? – had dropped three large white pines across each other. They were dead now, dry and filled with weathered dry dead limbs – enough for many days. He chopped and broke and carried wood back to the camp, stacking the pieces under the overhang until he had what he thought to be an enormous pile, as high as his head and six feet across the base. Between trips he added small pieces to the fire to keep it going and on one of the trips to get wood he noticed an added advantage of the fire. When he was in the shade of the trees breaking limbs the mosquitoes swarmed on him, as usual, but when he came to the fire, or just near the shelter where the smoke eddied and swirled, the insects were gone.

It was a wonderful discovery. The mosquitoes had nearly driven him mad and the thought of being rid of them lifted his spirits. On another trip he looked back and saw the smoke curling up through the trees and realised, for the first time, that he now had the means to make a signal. He could carry a burning stick and build a signal fire on top of the rock, make clouds of smoke and perhaps attract attention.

Which meant more wood. And still more wood. There did not seem to be an end to the wood he would need and he spent all the rest of the afternoon into dusk making wood trips.

At dark he settled in again for the night, next to the fire with the stack of short pieces ready to put on, and he ate the rest of the raspberries. During all the work of the day his leg had loosened but it still ached a bit, and he rubbed it and watched the fire and thought for the first time since the crash that he might be getting a handle on things, might be starting to do something other than just sit.

He was out of food, but he could look tomorrow and he could build a signal fire tomorrow and get more wood tomorrow . . .

The fire cut the night coolness and settled him back into sleep, thinking of tomorrow.

He slept hard and wasn't sure what awakened him but his eyes came open and he stared into the darkness. The fire had burned down and looked out but he stirred with a piece of wood and found a bed of coals still glowing hot and red. With small pieces of wood and careful blowing he soon had a blaze going again.

It had been close. He had to be sure to try and sleep in short intervals so he could keep the fire going, and he tried to think of a way to regulate his sleep but it made him sleepy to think about it and he was just going under again when he heard the sound outside.

It was not unlike the sound of the porcupine, something slithering and being dragged across the sand, but when he looked out of the door opening it was too dark to see anything.

Whatever it was it stopped making that sound in a few moments and he thought he heard something sloshing into the water at the shoreline, but he had the fire now and plenty of wood so he wasn't as worried as he had been the night before.

He dozed, slept for a time, awakened again just at dawn-grey light, and added wood to the still-smoking fire before standing outside and stretching. Standing with his arms stretched over his head and the tight knot of hunger in his stomach, he looked towards the lake and saw the tracks.

They were strange, a main centre line up from the lake in the sand with claw marks to the side leading to a small pile of sand, then going back down to the water.

He walked over and squatted near them, studied them, tried to make sense of them.

Whatever had made the tracks had some kind of flat dragging bottom in the middle and was apparently pushed along by the legs that stuck out to the side.

Up from the water to a small pile of sand, then back down into the water. Some animal. Some kind of water animal that came up to the sand to . . . to do what?

To do something with the sand, to play and make a pile in the sand?

He smiled. City boy, he thought. Oh, you city boy with your city ways – he made a mirror in his mind, a mirror of himself, and saw how he must look. City boy with your city ways sitting in the sand trying to read the tracks and not knowing, not understanding. Why would anything wild come up from the water to play in the sand? Not that way, animals weren't that way. They didn't waste time that way.

It had come up from the water for a reason, a good reason, and he must try to understand the reason, he must change to fully understand the reason himself or he would not make it.

It had come up from the water for a reason, and the reason, he thought, squatting, the reason had to do with the pile of sand.

He brushed the top off gently with his hand but

78

found only damp sand. Still, there must be a reason and he carefully kept scraping and digging until, about four inches down, he suddenly came into a small chamber in the cool-damp sand and there lay eggs, many eggs, almost perfectly round eggs the size of table-tennis balls, and he laughed then because he knew.

It had been a turtle. He had seen a programme on television about sea turtles that came up on to beaches and laid their eggs in the sand. There must be freshwater lake turtles that did the same. Maybe snapping turtles. He had heard of snapping turtles. They became fairly large, he thought. It must have been a snapper that came up in the night when he heard the noise that woke him; she must have come then and laid the eggs.

Food.

More than eggs, more than knowledge, more than anything this was food. His stomach tightened and rolled and made noise as he looked at the eggs, as if his stomach belonged to somebody else or had seen the eggs with its own eyes and was demanding food. The hunger, always there, had been somewhat controlled and dormant when there was nothing to eat but with the eggs came the scream to eat. His whole body craved food with such an intensity that it quickened his breath.

He reached into the nest and pulled the eggs out one at a time. There were seventeen of them, each as round as a ball, and white. They had leathery shells that gave instead of breaking when he squeezed them.

When he had them heaped on the sand in a pyramid – he had never felt so rich somehow – he

79

suddenly realised that he did not know how to eat them.

He had a fire but no way to cook them, no container, and he had never thought of eating a raw egg. He had an uncle named Carter, his father's brother, who always put an egg in a glass of milk and drank it in the morning. Brian had watched him do it once, just once, and when the runny part of the white left the glass and went into his uncle's mouth and down the throat in a single gulp Brian almost lost everything he had ever eaten.

Still, he thought. Still. As his stomach moved towards his backbone he became less and less fussy. Some natives in the world ate grasshoppers and ants and if they could do that he could get a raw egg down.

He picked one up and tried to break the shell and found it surprisingly tough. Finally, using the hatchet he sharpened a stick and poked a hole in the egg. He widened the hole with his finger and looked inside. Just an egg. It had a dark yellow yolk and not so much white as he thought there would be.

Just an egg.

Food.

Just an egg he had to eat.

Raw.

He looked out across the lake and brought the egg to his mouth and closed his eyes and sucked and squeezed the egg at the same time and swallowed as fast as he could.

'Ecch . . .'

It had a greasy, almost oily taste, but it was still an egg. His throat tried to throw it back up, his whole body seemed to convulse with it, but his stomach took it, held it, and demanded more.

The second egg was easier, and by the third one he had no trouble at all – it just slid down. He ate six of them, could have easily eaten all of them and not been full, but a part of him said to hold back, save the rest.

He could not now believe the hunger. The eggs had awakened it fully, roaringly, so that it tore at him. After the sixth egg he ripped the shell open and licked the inside clean, then went back and ripped the other five open and licked them out as well and wondered if he could eat the shells. There must be some food value in them. But when he tried they were too leathery to chew and he couldn't get them down.

He stood away from the eggs for a moment, literally stood and turned away so that he could not see them. If he looked at them he would have to eat more.

He would store them in the shelter and eat only one a day. He fought the hunger down again, controlled it. He would take them now and store them and save them and eat one a day, and he realised as he thought it that he had forgotten that *they* might come. The searchers. Surely, they would come before he could eat all the eggs at one a day.

He had forgotten to think about them and that wasn't good. He had to keep thinking of them because if he forgot them and did not think of them they might forget about him.

And he had to keep hoping.

He had to keep hoping.

ELEVEN

There were these things to do.

He transferred all the eggs from the small beach into the shelter, reburying them near his sleeping area. It took all his will to keep from eating another one as he moved them, but he got it done and when they were out of sight again it was easier. He added wood to the fire and cleaned up the camp area.

A good laugh, that – cleaning the camp. All he did was shake out his anorak and hang it in the sun to dry the berry juice that had soaked in, and smooth the sand where he slept.

But it was a mental thing. He had got depressed thinking about how they hadn't found him yet, and when he was busy and had something to do the depression seemed to leave.

So there were things to do.

With the camp squared away he brought in more wood. He had decided to always have enough on hand for three days and after spending one night with the fire for a friend he knew what a staggering amount of wood it would take. He worked all through the morning at the wood, breaking down dead limbs and breaking or chopping them in smaller pieces, storing them neatly beneath the overhang. He stopped once to take a drink at the lake and in his reflection he saw that the swelling on his head was nearly gone. There was no pain there so he assumed that had taken care of itself. His leg was also back to normal, although he had a small pattern of holes – roughly star-shaped – where the quills had nailed him, and while he was standing at the lake shore taking stock he noticed that his body was changing.

He had never been fat, but he had been slightly heavy with a little extra weight just above his belt at the sides.

This was completely gone and his stomach had caved in to the hunger and the sun had cooked him past burning so he was tanning, and with the smoke from the fire his face was starting to look like leather. But perhaps more than his body was the change in his mind, or in the way he was – was becoming.

I am not the same, he thought. I see, I hear differently. He did not know when the change started, but it was there; when a sound came to him now he didn't just hear it but would know the sound. He would swing and look at it – a breaking twig, a movement of air – and know the sound as if he somehow could move his mind back down the wave of sound to the source.

He could know what the sound was before he quite realised he had heard it. And when he saw something – a bird moving a wing inside a bush or a ripple on the water – he would truly see that thing, not just notice it as he used to notice things in the city. He would see all parts of it; see the whole wing, the feathers, see the colour of the feathers, see the bush, and the size and shape and colour of its leaves. He would see the way the light moved with the ripples on the water and see that the wind made the ripples and which way that wind had to blow to make the ripples move in that certain way.

None of that used to be in Brian and now it was a part of him, a changed part of him, a grown part of him, and the two things, his mind and his body, had come together as well, had made a connection with each other that he didn't quite understand. When his ears heard a sound or his eyes saw a sight his mind took control of his body. Without his thinking, he moved to face the sound or sight, moved to make ready for it, to deal with it.

There were these things to do.

When the wood was done he decided to get a signal fire ready. He moved to the top of the rock ridge that comprised the bluff over his shelter and was pleased to find a large, flat stone area.

More wood, he thought, moaning inwardly. He went back to the fallen trees and found more dead limbs, carrying them up on the rock until he had enough for a bonfire. Initially he had thought of making a signal fire every day but he couldn't – he would never be able to keep the wood supply going. So while he was working he decided to have the fire ready and if he heard an engine, or even thought he heard a plane engine, he would run up with a burning limb and set off the signal fire.

Things to do.

At the last trip to the top of the stone bluff with wood he stopped, sat on the point overlooking the lake, and rested. The lake lay before him, twenty or so feet below, and he had not seen it this way since he had come in with the plane. Remembering the crash he had a moment of fear, a breath-tightening little rip of terror, but it passed and he was quickly caught up in the beauty of the scenery.

It was so incredibly beautiful that it was almost

unreal. From his height he could see not just the lake but across part of the forest, a green carpet, and it was full of life. Birds, insects – there was a constant hum and song. At the other end of the bottom of the L there was another large rock sticking out over the water and on top of the rock a snaggly pine had somehow found food and grown, bent and gnarled. Sitting on one limb was a blue bird with a crest and sharp beak, a kingfisher – he thought of a picture he had seen once – which left the branch while he watched and dived into the water. It emerged a split part of a second later. In its mouth was a small fish, wiggling silver in the sun. It took the fish to a limb, juggled it twice, and swallowed it whole.

Fish.

Of course, he thought. There were fish in the lake and they were food. And if a bird could do it . . .

He scrambled down the side of the bluff and trotted to the edge of the lake, looking down into the water. Somehow it had never occurred to him to look *inside* the water – only at the surface. The sun was flashing back up into his eyes and he moved off to the side and took his shoes off and waded out fifteen feet. Then he turned and stood still, with the sun at his back, and studied the water again.

It was, he saw after a moment, literally packed with life. Small fish swam everywhere, some narrow and long, some round, most of them three or four inches long, some a bit larger and many smaller. There was a patch of mud off to the side, leading into deeper water, and he could see old clam shells there, so there must be clams. As he watched, a crayfish, looking like a tiny lobster, left one of the empty

85

clam shells and went to another looking for something to eat, digging with its claws.

While he stood some of the small, roundish fish came quite close to his legs and he tensed, got ready, and made a wild stab at grabbing one of them. They exploded away in a hundred flicks of quick light, so fast that he had no hope of catching them that way. But they soon came back, seemed to be curious about him, and as he walked from the water he tried to think of a way to use that curiosity to catch them.

He had no hooks or string but if he could somehow lure them into the shallows – and make a spear, a small fish spear – he might be able to strike fast enough to get one.

He would have to find the right kind of wood, slim and straight – he had seen some willows up along the lake that might work – and he could use the hatchet to sharpen it and shape it while he was sitting by the fire tonight. And that brought up the fire, which he had to feed again. He looked at the sun and saw it was getting late in the afternoon, and when he thought of how late it was he thought that he ought to reward all his work with another egg and that made him think that some kind of dessert would be nice – he smiled when he thought of dessert, so fancy – and he wondered if he should move up the lake and see if he could find some raspberries after he banked the fire and while he was looking for the right wood for a spear. Spearwood, he thought, and it all rolled together, just rolled together and rolled over him . . .

There were these things to do.

TWELVE

The fish spear didn't work.

He stood in the shallows and waited, again and again. The small fish came closer and closer and he lunged time after time but was always too slow. He tried throwing it, jabbing it, everything but flailing with it, and it didn't work. The fish were just too fast.

He had been so sure, so absolutely certain that it would work the night before. Sitting by the fire he had taken the willow and carefully peeled the bark until he had a straight staff about six feet long and just under an inch thick at the base, the thickest end.

Then, propping the hatchet in a crack in the rock wall, he had pulled the head of his spear against it, carving a thin piece off each time, until the thick end tapered down to a needle point. Still not satisfied – he could not imagine hitting one of the fish with a single point – he carefully used the hatchet to split the point up the middle for eight or ten inches and jammed a piece of wood up into the split to make a two-prong spear with the points about two inches apart. It was crude, but it looked effective and seemed to have good balance when he stood outside the shelter and hefted the spear.

He had worked on the fish spear until it had become more than just a tool. He'd spent hours and hours on it, and now it didn't work. He moved into the shallows and stood and the fish came to him. Just as before they swarmed around his legs, some of them almost six inches long, but no matter how he tried they were too fast. At first he tried throwing it but that had no chance. As soon as he brought his arm back – well before he threw – the movement frightened them. Next he tried lunging at them, having the spear ready just above the water and thrusting with it. Finally he actually put the spear in the water and waited until the fish were right in front of it, but still somehow he telegraphed his motion before he thrust and they saw it and flashed away.

He needed something to spring the spear forward, some way to make it move faster than the fish – some motive force. A string that snapped – or a bow. A bow and arrow. A thin, long arrow with the point in the water and the bow pulled back so that all he had to do was release the arrow . . . yes. That was it.

He had to 'invent' the bow and arrow – he almost laughed as he moved out of the water and put his shoes on. The morning sun was getting hot and he took his shirt off. Maybe that was how it really happened, way back when – some primitive man tried to spear fish and it didn't work and he 'invented' the bow and arrow. Maybe it was always that way, discoveries happened because they needed to happen.

He had not eaten anything yet this morning so he took a moment to dig up the eggs and eat one. Then he reburied them, banked the fire with a couple of thicker pieces of wood, settled the hatchet on his belt and took the spear in his right hand and set off up the lake to find wood to make a bow. He went without a shirt but something about the wood smoke smell on him kept the insects from bothering him as he walked to the berry patch. The raspberries were staring to become overripe, just in two days, and he would have to pick as many as possible after he found the wood but he did take a little time now to pick a few and eat them. They were full and sweet and when he picked one, two others would fall off the limbs into the grass and soon his hands and cheeks were covered with red berry juice and he was full. That surprised him – being full.

He hadn't thought he would ever be full again, knew only the hunger, and here he was full. One turtle egg and a few handfuls of berries and he felt full. He looked down at his stomach and saw that it was still caved in – did not bulge out as it would have with two hamburgers and a milkshake. It must have shrunk. And there was still hunger there, but not like it was – not tearing at him. This was hunger that he knew would be there always, even when he had food – a hunger that made him look for things, see things. A hunger to make him hunt.

He swung his eyes across the berries to make sure the bear wasn't there, at his back, then he moved down to the lake. The spear went out before him automatically, moving the brush away from his face as he walked, and when he came to the water's edge he swung left. Not sure what he was looking for, not knowing what wood might be best for a bow – he had never made a bow, never shot a bow in his life – but it seemed that it would be along the lake, near the water.

He saw some young birch, and they were springy, but they lacked snap somehow, as did the willows. Not enough whip-back.

Halfway up the lake, just as he started to step over

a log, he was absolutely terrified by an explosion under his feet. Something like a feathered bomb blew up and away in a flurry of leaves and thunder. It frightened him so badly that he fell back and down and then it was gone, leaving only an image in his mind.

A bird, it had been, about the size of a very small chicken only with a fantail and stubby wings that slammed against its body and made a loud noise. Noise there and gone. He got up and brushed himself off. The bird had been speckled, brown and grey, and it must not be very smart because Brian's foot had been nearly on it before it flew. Half a second more and he would have stepped on it.

And caught it, he thought, and eaten it. He might be able to catch one, or spear one. Maybe, he thought, maybe it tasted like chicken. Maybe he could catch one or spear one and it probably did taste just like chicken. Just like chicken when his mother roasted it in the oven with garlic and salt and it turned golden brown and crackled . . .

He shook his head to drive the picture out and moved down to the shore. There was a tree there with long branches that seemed straight and when he pulled on one of them and let go it had an almost vicious snap to it. He picked one of the limbs that seemed right and began chopping where the limb joined the tree.

The wood was hard and he didn't want to cause it to split so he took his time, took small chips and concentrated so hard that at first he didn't hear it.

A persistent whine, like the insects only more steady with an edge of a roar to it, was in his ears and he chopped and cut and was thinking of a bow, how he would make a bow, how it would be when he shaped it with the hatchet and still the sound did not cut through until the limb was nearly off the tree and the whine was inside his head and he knew it then.

A plane! It was a motor, far off but seeming to get louder. They were coming for him!

He threw down the limb and his spear and, holding the hatchet, started to run for camp. He had to get fire up on the bluff and signal them, get fire and smoke up. He put all of his life into his legs, jumped logs and moved through brush like a light ghost, swivelling and running, his lungs filling and blowing and now the sound was louder, coming in his direction.

If not right at him, at least closer. He could see it all in his mind now, the picture, the way it would be. He would get the fire going and the plane would see the smoke and circle, circle once, then again, and waggle its wings. It would be a float plane and it would land on the water and come across the lake and the pilot would be amazed that he was alive after all these days.

All this he saw as he ran for the camp and the fire. They would take him from here and this night, this very night, he would sit with his father and eat and tell him all the things. He could see it now. Oh, yes, all as he ran in the sun, his legs liquid springs. He got to the camp still hearing the whine of the engine, and one stock of wood still had good flame.

He dived inside and grabbed the wood and ran around the edge of the ridge, scrambled up like a cat and blew and nearly had the flame feeding, growing, when the sound moved away.

It was abrupt, as if the plane had turned. He shielded the sun from his eyes and tried to see it, tried to make the plane become real in his eyes. But the trees were so high, so thick, and now the sound was still fainter. He kneeled again to the flames and blew and added grass and chips and the flames fed and grew and in moments he had a bonfire as high as his head but the sound was gone now.

Look back, he thought. Look back and see the smoke now and turn, please turn.

'Look back,' he whispered, feeling all the pictures fade, seeing his father's face fade like the sound, like lost dreams, like an end to hope. Oh, turn now and come back, look back and see the smoke and turn for me . . .

But it kept moving away until he could not hear it even in his imagination, in his soul. Gone. He stood on the bluff over the lake, his face cooking in the roaring bonfire, watching the clouds of ash and smoke going into the sky and thought – no, more than thought – he knew then that he would not get out of this place. Not now, not ever.

That had been a search plane. He was sure of it. That must have been them and they had come as far off to the side of the flight plan as they thought they would have to come and then turned back. They did not see his smoke, did not hear the cry from his mind.

They would not return. He would never leave now, never get out of here. He went down to his knees and felt the tears start, cutting through the smoke and ash on his face, silently falling on to the stone.

Gone, he thought finally, it was all gone. All silly and gone. No bows, no spears, or fish or berries, it was all silly anyway, all just a game. He could do a day, but not for ever – he could not make it if they did not come for him some day.

He could not play the game without hope; could not play the game without a dream. They had taken it all away from him now, they had turned away from him and there was nothing for him now. The plane gone, his family gone, all of it gone. They would not come. He was alone and there was nothing for him.

THIRTEEN

Brian stood at the end of the long part of the L of the lake and watched the water, smelled the water, listened to the water, was the water.

A fish moved and his eyes jerked sideways to see the ripples but he did not move any other part of his body and did not raise the bow or reach into his belt pouch for a fish arrow. It was not the right kind of fish, not a food fish.

The food fish stayed close in, in the shallows, and did not roll that way but made quicker movements, small movements, food movements. The large fish rolled and stayed deep and could not be taken. But it didn't matter. This day, this morning, he was not looking for fish. Fish was light meat and he was sick of them.

He was looking for one of the foolish birds – he called them foolbirds – and there was a flock that lived near the end of the long part of the lake. But something he did not understand had stopped him and be stood, breathing gently through his mouth to keep silent, letting his eyes and ears go out and do the work for him.

It had happened before this way, something had come into him from outside to warn him and he had stopped. Once it had been the bear again. He had been taking the last of the raspberries and something came inside and stopped him, and when he looked where his ears said to look there was a female bear with cubs.

Had he taken two more steps he would have come between the mother and her cubs and that was a bad place to be. As it was the mother had stood and faced him and made a sound, a low sound in her throat to threaten and warn him. He paid attention to the feeling now and he stood and waited, patiently, knowing he was right and that something would come.

Turn, smell, listen, feel and then a sound, a small sound, and he looked up and away from the lake and saw the wolf. It was halfway up the hill from the lake, standing with its head and shoulders sticking out into a small opening, looking down on him with wide yellow eyes. He had never seen a wolf and the size threw him – not as big as a bear but somehow seeming that large. The wolf claimed all that was below him as his own, took Brian as his own.

Brian looked back and for a moment felt afraid because the wolf was so . . . so right. He knew Brian, knew him and owned him and chose not to do anything to him. But the fear moved then, moved away, and Brian knew the wolf for what it was – another part of the woods, another part of all of it. Brian relaxed the tension on the spear in his hand, settled the bow in his other hand from where it had started to come up. He knew the wolf now, as the wolf knew him, and he nodded to it, nodded and smiled.

The wolf watched him for another time, another part of his life, then it turned and walked effortlessly up the hill and as it came out of the brush it was followed by three other wolves, all equally large and grey and beautiful, all looking down on him as they

95

trotted past and away and Brian nodded to each of them.

He was not the same now – the Brian that stood and watched the wolves move away and nodded to them was completely changed. Time had come, time that he measured but didn't care about; time had come into his life and moved out and left him different.

In measured time forty-seven days had passed since the crash. Forty-two days, he thought, since he had died and been born as the new Brian.

When the plane had come and gone it had put him down, gutted him and dropped him and left him with nothing. The rest of that first day he had gone down and down until dark. He had let the fire go out, had forgotten to eat even an egg, had let his brain take him down to where he was done, where he wanted to be done and done.

To where he wanted to die. He had settled into the grey funk deeper and still deeper until finally, in the dark, he had gone up on the ridge and taken the hatchet and tried to end it by cutting himself.

Madness. A hissing madness that took his brain. There had been nothing for him then and he tried to become nothing but the cutting had been hard to do, impossible to do, and he had at last fallen to his side, wishing for death, wishing for an end, and slept only didn't sleep.

With his eyes closed and his mind open he lay on the rock through the night, lay and hated and wished for it to end and thought the word *Clouddown, Clouddown* through that awful night. Over and over the word, wanting all his clouds to come down, but in the morning he was still there.

Still there on his side and the sun came up and when he opened his eyes he saw the cuts on his arm, the dry blood turning black; he saw the blood and hated the blood, hated what he had done to himself when he was the old Brian and was weak, and the two things came into his mind – two true things.

He was not the same. The plane passing changed him, the disappointment cut him down and made him new. He was not the same and would never be again like he had been. That was one of the true things, the new things. And the other one was that he would not die, he would not let death in again.

He was new.

Of course he had made a lot of mistakes. He smiled now, walking up the lake shore after the wolves were gone, thinking of the early mistakes; the mistakes that came before he realised that he had to find new ways to be what he had become.

He had made new fire, which he now kept going using partially rotten wood because the punky wood would smoulder for many hours and still come back with fire. But that had been the extent of doing things right for a while. His first bow was a disaster that almost blinded him.

He had sat a whole night and shaped the limbs carefully until the bow looked beautiful. Then he had spent two days making arrows. The shafts were willow, straight and with the bark peeled, and he fire-hardened the points and split a couple of them to make forked points, as he had done with the spear. He had no feathers so he just left them bare, figuring for fish they only had to travel a few inches. He had no string and that threw him until he looked down at his tennis shoes. They had long laces, too long, and he found that one lace cut in half would take care of both shoes and that left the other lace for a bowstring.

All seemed to be going well until he tried a test shot. He put an arrow to the string, pulled it back to his cheek, pointed it at a dirt hummock, and at that precise instant the bow wood exploded in his hands sending splinters and chips of wood into his face. Two pieces actually stuck into his forehead, just above his eyes, and had they been only slightly lower they would have blinded him.

Too stiff.

Mistakes. In his mental journal he listed them to tell his father, listed all the mistakes. He had made a new bow, with slender limbs and a more fluid, gentle pull, but could not hit the fish though he sat in the water and was, in the end, surrounded by a virtual cloud of small fish. It was infuriating. He would pull the bow back, set the arrow just above the water, and when the fish was no more than an inch away release the arrow.

Only to miss. It seemed to him that the arrow had gone right through the fish, again and again, but the fish didn't get hurt. Finally, after hours, he stuck the arrow down in the water, pulled the bow, and waited for a fish to come close and while he was waiting he noticed that the water seemed to make the arrow bend or break in the middle.

Of course – he had forgotten that water refracts, bends light. He had learned that somewhere, in some class, maybe it was biology – he couldn't remember. But it did bend light and that meant the fish were not where they appeared to be. They were lower, just below, which meant he had to aim just under them.

He would not forget his first hit. Not ever. A round-shaped fish, with golden sides, sides as gold as the sun, stopped in front of the arrow and he aimed just beneath it, at the bottom edge of the fish, and released the arrow and there was a bright flurry, a splash of gold in the water. He grabbed the arrow and raised it up and the fish was on the end, wiggling against the blue sky.

He held the fish against the sky until it stopped wiggling, held it and looked to the sky and felt his throat tighten, swell, and fill with pride at what he had done.

He had done food.

With his bow, with an arrow fashioned by his own hands he had done food, had found a way to live. The bow had given him this way and he exulted in it, in the bow, in the arrow, in the fish, in the hatchet, in the sky. He stood and walked from the water, still holding the fish and arrow and bow against the sky, seeing them as they fitted his arms, as they were part of him.

He had food.

He cut a green willow fork and held the fish over the fire until the skin crackled and peeled away and the meat inside was flaky and moist and tender. This he picked off carefully with his fingers, tasting every piece, mashing them in his mouth with his tongue to get the juices out of them, hot steaming pieces of fish . . .

He could not, he thought then, ever get enough. And all that first day, first new day, he spent going to the lake, shooting a fish, taking it back to the fire, cooking it and eating it, then back to the lake, shooting a fish, cooking it and eating it, and on that way until it was dark.

He had taken the scraps back to the water with the thought they might work for bait, and the other fish came by the hundreds to clean them up. He could take his pick of them. Like a store, he thought, just like a store, and he could not remember later how many he ate that day but he thought it must have been over twenty.

It had been a feast day, his first feast day, and a celebration of being alive and the new way he had of getting food. By the end of that day, when it became dark and he lay next to the fire with his stomach full of fish and grease from the meat smeared around his mouth, he could feel new hope building in him. Not hope that he would be rescued – that was gone.

But hope in his knowledge. Hope in the fact that he could learn and survive and take care of himself.

Tough hope, he thought that night. I am full of tough hope.

FOURTEEN

Mistakes.

Small mistakes could turn into disasters, funny little mistakes could snowball so that while you were still smiling at the humour you could find yourself looking at death. In the city if he made a mistake usually there was a way to rectify it, make it all right. If he fell on his bike and sprained a leg he could wait for it to heal; if he forgot something at the shop he could find other food in the refrigerator.

Now it was different, and all so quick, all so incredibly quick. If he sprained a leg here he might starve before he could get around again; if he missed while he was hunting or if the fish moved away he might starve. If he got sick, really sick so he couldn't move, he might starve.

Mistakes.

Early in the new time he had learned the most important thing, the truly vital knowledge that drives all creatures in the forest – food is all. Food was simply everything. All things in the woods, from insects to fish to bears, were always, always looking for food – it was the great, single driving influence in nature. To eat. All must eat.

But the way he learned it almost killed him. His second new night, stomach full of fish and the fire smouldering in the shelter, he had been sound asleep when something – he thought later it might be smell – had woken him.

Near the fire, completely unafraid of the smoking logs, completely unafraid of Brian, a skunk was digging where he had buried the eggs. There was some sliver of a moon and in the faint-pearl light he could see the bushy tail, the white stripes down the back, and he had nearly smiled. He did not know how the skunk had found the eggs, some smell, perhaps some tiny fragment of shell had left a smell, but it looked almost cute, its little head down and its little tail up as it dug and dug, kicking the sand back.

But those were his eggs, not the skunk's, and the half smile had been quickly replaced with fear that he would lose his food and he had grabbed a handful of sand and thrown it at the skunk.

'Get out of here . . .'

He was going to say more, some silly human words, but in less than half a second the skunk had snapped its rear end up, curved the tail over, and sprayed Brian with a direct shot aimed at his head from less than four feet away.

In the tiny confines of the shelter the effect was devastating. The thick sulphurous rotten odour filled the small room, heavy, ugly and stinking. The corrosive spray that hit his face seared into his lungs and eyes, blinding him.

He screamed and threw himself sideways, taking the entire wall off the shelter; screamed and clawed out of the shelter and fell-ran to the shore of the lake. Stumbling and tripping, he scrambled into the water and slammed his head back and forth trying to wash his eyes, slashing at the water to clear his eyes.

A hundred funny cartoons he had seen about skunks. Cute cartoons about the smell of skunks, cartoons to laugh at and joke about, but when the spray hit there was nothing funny about it – he was completely blind for almost two hours. A lifetime. He thought that he might be permanently blind, or at least impaired – and that would have been the end. As it was the pain in his eyes lasted for days, bothered him after that for two weeks. The smell in the shelter, in his clothes, and in his hair was still there now, almost a month and a half later.

And he had nearly smiled.

Mistakes.

Food had to be protected. While he was in the lake trying to clear his eyes the skunk went ahead and dug up the rest of the turtle eggs and ate every one. Licked all the shells clean and couldn't have cared less that Brian was thrashing around in the water like a dying carp. The skunk had found food and was taking it and Brian was paying for a lesson.

Protect food and have a good shelter. Not just a shelter to keep the wind and rain out, but a shelter to protect, a shelter to make him safe. The day after the skunk he set about making a good place to live.

The basic idea had been good, the place for his shelter was right, but he just hadn't gone far enough. He'd been lazy – but now he knew the second most important thing about nature, what drives nature. Food was first, but the work for the food went on and on. Nothing in nature was lazy. He had tried to take a short cut and paid for it with his turtle eggs – which he had come to like more than chicken eggs from the shop. They were fuller somehow, had more depth to them.

He set about improving his shelter by tearing it down. From dead pines up the hill he brought down heavier logs and fastened several of them across the opening, wedging them at the top and burying the bottoms in the sand. Then he wove long branches in through them to make a truly tight wall and, still not satisfied, he took even thinner branches and wove those into the first weave. When he was at last finished he could not find a place to put his fist through. It all held together like a very stiff woven basket.

He judged the door opening to be the weakest spot, and here he took special time to weave a door of willows in so tight a mesh that no matter how a skunk tried – or porcupine, he thought, looking at the marks in his leg – it could not possibly get through. He had no hinges but by arranging some cut-off limbs at the top in the right way he had a method to hook the door in place, and when he was in and the door was hung he felt relatively safe. A bear, something big, could still get in by tearing at it, but nothing small could bother him and the weave of the structure still allowed the smoke to filter up through the top and out.

All in all it took him three days to make the shelter, stopping to shoot fish and eat as he went, bathing four times a day to try and get the smell from the skunk to leave. When his house was done, finally done right, he turned to the constant problem – food.

It was all right to hunt and eat, or fish and eat, but what happened if he had to go a long time without food? What happened when the berries were gone and he got sick or hurt or – thinking of the skunk – laid up temporarily? He needed a way to store food, a place to store it, and he needed food to store.

Mistakes.

He tried to learn from the mistakes. He couldn't bury food again, couldn't leave it in the shelter, because something like a bear could get at it right away. It had to be high, somehow, high and safe. Above the door to the shelter, up the rock face about ten feet, was a small ledge that could make a natural storage place, unreachable to animals – except that it was unreachable to him as well.

A ladder, of course. He needed a ladder. But he had no way to fashion one, nothing to hold the steps on, and that stopped him until he found a dead pine with many small branches still sticking out. Using his hatchet he chopped the branches off so they stuck out four or five inches, all up along the log, then he cut the log off about ten feet long and dragged it down to his shelter. It was a little heavy, but dry and he could manage it, and when he propped it up he found he could climb to the ledge with ease, though the tree did roll from side to side a bit as he climbed.

His food shelf – as he thought of it – had been covered with bird manure and he carefully scraped it clean with sticks. He had never seen birds there, but that was probably because the smoke from his fire went up right across the opening and they didn't like smoke. Still, he had learned and he took time to weave a snug door for the small opening with green willows, cutting it so it jammed in tightly, and when he finished he stood back and looked at the rock face – his shelter below, the food shelf above – and allowed a small bit of pride to come.

Not bad, he had thought, not bad for somebody

105

who used to have trouble greasing the bearings on his bicycle. Not bad at all.

Mistakes.

He had made a good shelter and food shelf, but he had no food except for fish and the last of the berries. And the fish, as good as they still tasted then, were not something he could store. His mother had left some salmon out by mistake one time when they went on an overnight trip to Cape Hesper to visit relatives and when they got back the smell filled the whole house. There was no way to store fish.

At least, he thought, no way to store them dead. But as he looked at the weave of his structure a brought came to him and he moved down to the water.

He had been putting the waste from the fish back in the water and the food had attracted hundreds of new ones.

'I wonder . . .'

They seemed to come easily to the food, at least the small ones. He had no trouble now shooting them and had even speared one with his old fish spear now that he knew to aim low. He could dangle something in his fingers and they came right up to it. It might be possible, he thought, might just be possible to trap them. Make some kind of pond . . .

To his right, at the base of the rock bluff, there were piles of smaller rocks that had fallen from the main chunk, splinters and hunks, from double-fist size to some as large as his head. He spent an afternoon carrying rocks to the beach and making what amounted to a large pen for holding live fish – two rock 'arms' that stuck out fifteen feet into the lake and curved together at the end. Where the arms came together he left an opening about two feet across; then he sat on the shore and waited.

When he had first started dropping the rocks all the fish had darted away. But his fish-trash pile of bones and skin and guts was in the pond area and the prospect of food brought them back. Soon, in under an hour, there were thirty or forty small fish in the enclosure and Brian made a gate by weaving small willows together into a fine mesh and closed them in.

'Fresh fish,' he had yelled. 'I have fresh fish for sale . . .'

Storing live fish to eat later had been a major breakthrough, he thought. It wasn't just keeping from starving – it was trying to save ahead, think ahead.

Of course he didn't know then how sick he would get of fish.

FIFTEEN

The days had folded one into another and mixed so that after two or three weeks he only knew time had passed in days because he made a mark for each day in the stone near the door to his shelter. Real time he measured in events. A day was nothing, not a thing to remember – it was just sun coming up, sun going down, some light in the middle.

But events – events were burned into his memory and so he used them to remember time, to know and to remember what had happened, to keep a mental journal.

There had been the day of First Meat. That had been a day that had started like the rest, up after the sun, clean the camp and make sure there is enough wood for another night. But it was a long time, a long time of eating fish and looking for berries, and he craved more, craved more food, heavier food, deeper food.

He craved meat. He thought in the night now of meat, thought of his mother's cooking a roast or dreamed of turkey, and one night he awakened before he had to put wood on the fire with his mouth making saliva and the taste of pork chops in his mouth. So real, so real. And all a dream, but it left him intent on getting meat.

He had been working further and further out for wood, sometimes now going nearly a quarter of a mile away from camp for wood, and he saw many small animals. Squirrels were everywhere, small red ones that chattered at him and seemed to swear and jumped from limb to limb. There were also many rabbits – large, grey ones with a mix of reddish fur, smaller fast grey ones that he saw only at dawn. The larger ones sometimes sat until he was quite close, then bounded and jerked two or three steps before freezing again. He thought if he worked at it and practised he might hit one of the larger rabbits with an arrow or a spear – never the small ones or the squirrels. They were too small and fast.

Then there were the foolbirds.

They exasperated him to the point where they were close to driving him insane. The birds were everywhere, five and six in a flock, and their camouflage was so perfect that it was possible for Brian to sit and rest, leaning against a tree, with one of them standing right in front of him in a willow clump, two feet away – hidden – only to explode into deafening flight just when Brian least expected it. He just couldn't see them, couldn't figure out how to locate them before they flew, because they stood so perfectly still and blended in so perfectly well.

And what made it worse was that they were so dumb, or seemed to be so dumb, that it was almost insulting the way they kept hidden from him. Nor could he get used to the way they exploded up when they flew. It seemed like every time he went for wood, which was every morning, he spent the whole time jumping and jerking in fright as he walked. On one memorable morning he had actually reached for a piece of wood, what he thought to be a pitchy stump at the base of a dead birch, his fingers close to touching it, only to have it blow up in his face.

But on the day of First Meat he had decided the best thing to try for would be a foolbird and that morning he had set out with his bow and spear to get one; to stay with it until he got one and ate some meat. Not to get wood, not to find berries, but to get a bird and eat some meat.

At first the hunt had not gone well. He saw plenty of birds, working up along the shore of the lake to the end, then down the other side, but he only saw them after they flew. He had to find a way to see them first, see them and get close enough to either shoot them with the bow or use the spear, and he could not find a way to see them.

When he had gone halfway round the lake, and had jumped up twenty or so birds, he finally gave up and sat at the base of a tree. He had to work this out, see what he was doing wrong. There were birds there, and he had eyes – he just had to bring the two things together.

Looking wrong, he thought. I am looking wrong. More, more than that I am being wrong somehow – I am doing it the wrong way. Fine – sarcasm came into his thoughts – I know that, thank you. I know I'm doing it wrong. But what is right? The morning sun had cooked him until it seemed his brain was frying, sitting by the tree, but nothing came until he got up and started to walk again and hadn't gone two steps when a bird got up. It had been there all the time, while he was thinking about how to see them, right next to him – right there.

He almost screamed.

But this time, when the bird flew, something caught

110

his eye and it was the secret key. The bird cut down towards the lake, then, seeing it couldn't land in the water, turned and flew back up the hill into the trees. When it turned, curving through the trees, the sun had caught it, and Brian, for an instant, saw it as a shape; sharp-pointed in front, back from the head in a streamlined bullet shape to the fat body.

Kind of like a pear, he had thought, with a point on one end and a fat little body; a flying pear.

And that had been the secret. He had been looking for feathers, for the colour of the bird, for a bird sitting there. He had to look for the outline instead, had to see the shape instead of the feathers or colour, had to train his eyes to see the shape . . .

It was like turning on a television. Suddenly he could see things he never saw before. In just moments, it seemed, he saw three birds before they flew, saw them sitting and got close to one of them, moving slowly, got close enough to try a shot with his bow.

He had missed that time, and had missed many more, but he saw them; he saw the little fat shapes with the pointed heads sitting in the brush all over the place. Time and again he drew, held, and let arrows fly but he still had no feathers on the arrows and they were little more than sticks that flopped out of the bow, sometimes going sideways. Even when a bird was seven or eight feet away the arrow would turn without feathers to stabilise it and hit brush or a twig. After a time he gave up with the bow. It had worked all right for the fish, when they came right to the end of the arrow, but it wasn't good for any kind of distance – at least not the way it was now.

But he had carried his fish spear, the original one

111

with the two prongs, and he moved the bow to his left hand and carried the spear in his right.

He tried throwing the spear but he was not good enough and not fast enough – the birds could fly amazingly fast, get up fast. But in the end he found that if he saw the bird sitting and moved sideways towards it – not directly towards it but at an angle, back and forth – he could get close enough to put the spear point out ahead almost to the bird and thrust-lunge with it. He came close twice, and then, down along the lake not far from the beaver house he got his first meat.

The bird had sat and he had lunged and the two points took the bird back down into the ground and killed it almost instantly – it had fluttered a bit – and Brian had grabbed it and held it in both hands until he was sure it was dead.

Then he picked up the spear and the bow and trotted back round the lake to his shelter, where the fire had burned down to glowing coals. He sat looking at the bird wondering what to do. With the fish, he had just cooked them whole, left everything in and picked the meat off. This was different; he would have to clean it.

It had always been so simple at home. He would go to the shop and get a chicken and it was all cleaned and neat, no feathers or insides, and his mother would roast it in the oven and he would eat it. His mother from the old time, from the time before, would bake it.

Now he had the bird, but he had never cleaned one, never taken the insides out or got rid of the feathers, and he didn't know where to start. But he wanted the meat – had to have the meat – and that drove him.

In the end the feathers came off easily. He tried to pluck them out but the skin was so fragile that it pulled off as well, so he just pulled the skin off the bird. Like peeling an orange, he thought, sort of. Except that when the skin was gone the insides fell out the back end.

He was immediately caught in a cloud of raw odour, a kind of steamy dung odour that came up from the greasy coil of insides that fell from the bird, and he nearly threw up. But there was something else to the smell as well, some kind of richness that went with his hunger and that overcame the sick smell.

He quickly cut the neck with his hatchet, cut the feet off the same way, and in his hand he held something like a small chicken with a dark, fat, thick breast and small legs.

He set it up on some sticks on the shelter wall and took the feathers and insides down to the water, to his fish pond. The fish would eat them, or eat what they could, and the feeding action would bring more fish. On second thoughts he took out the wing and tail feathers, which were stiff and long and pretty – banded and speckled in browns and greys and light reds. There might be some use for them, he thought, maybe work them on to the arrows somehow.

The rest he threw in the water, saw the small round fish begin tearing at it, and washed his hands. Back at the shelter the flies were on the meat and he brushed them off. It was amazing how fast they came, but when he build up the fire and the smoke increased the flies almost magically disappeared. He pushed a pointed stick through the bird and held it over the fire.

The fire was too hot. The flames hit the fat and the bird almost ignited. He held it higher but the heat was worse and finally he moved it to the side a bit and there it seemed to cook properly. Except that it only cooked on one side and all the juice dripped off. He had to rotate it slowly and that was hard to do with his hands so he found a forked stick and stuck it in the sand to put his cooking stick in. He turned it, and in this way he found a proper method to cook the bird.

In minutes the outside was cooked and the smell that came up was almost the same as the smell when his mother roasted chickens in the oven and he didn't think he could stand it but when he tried to pull a piece of the breast meat off the meat was still raw inside.

Patience, he thought. So much of this was patience – waiting and thinking and doing things right. So much of all this, so much of all living was patience and thinking.

He settled back, turning the bird slowly, letting the juices go back into the meat, letting it cook and smell and smell and cook and there came a time when it didn't matter if the meat was done or not; it was black on the outside and hard and hot, and he would eat it.

He tore a piece from the breast, a silver of meat, and put it in his mouth and chewed carefully, chewed as slowly and carefully as he could to get all the taste and he thought:

Never. Never in all the food, all the hamburgers and milkshakes, all the fries or meals at home, never in all the sweets or pies or cakes, never in all the roasts or steaks or pizzas, never never never had he tasted anything as fine as that first bite.

First Meat.

SIXTEEN

And now he stood at the end of the long part of the lake and was not the same, would not be the same again.

There had been many First Days.

First Arrow Day – when he had used thread from his tattered old piece of anorak and some pitch from a stump to put slivers of feather on a dry willow shaft and make an arrow that would fly correctly. Not accurately – he never got really good with it – but fly correctly so that if a rabbit or a foolbird sat in one place long enough, close enough, and he had enough arrows, he could hit it.

That brought First Rabbit Day – when he killed one of the large rabbits with an arrow and skinned it as he had the first bird, cooked it the same to find the meat as good – not as rich as the bird, but still good – and there were strips of fat on the back of the rabbit that cooked into the meat to make it richer.

Now he went back and forth between rabbits and foolbirds when he could, filling in with fish in the middle.

Always hungry.

I am always hungry but I can do it now, I can get food and I know I can get food and it makes me more. I know what I can do.

He moved closer to the lake to a stand of nut brush. These were thick bushes with little pods that

116

held green nuts – nuts that he thought he might be able to eat but they weren't ripe yet. He was out for a foolbird and they liked to hide in the base of the thick part of the nut brush, back in where the stems were close together and provided cover.

In the second clump he saw a bird, moved close to it, paused when the head feathers came up and it made a sound like a cricket – a sign of alarm just before it flew – then moved closer when the feathers went down and the bird relaxed. He did this four times, never looking at the bird directly, moving towards it at an angle so that it seemed he was moving off to the side – he had perfected this method after many attempts and it worked so well that he had actually caught one with his bare hands – until he was standing less than three feet from the bird, which was frozen in a hiding attitude in the brush.

The bird held for him and he put an arrow to the bow, one of the feathered arrows, not a fish arrow, and drew and released. It was a clean miss and he took another arrow out of the cloth pouch, at his belt, which he'd made from a piece of his anorak sleeve, tied at one end to make a bottom. The foolbird sat still for him and he did not look directly at it until he drew the second arrow and aimed and released and missed again.

This time the bird jerked a bit and the arrow stuck next to it so close it almost brushed its breast. Brian only had two more arrows and he debated moving slowly to change the spear over to his right hand and use that to kill the bird. One more shot, he decided, he would try it again. He slowly brought another arrow out, put it on the string, and aimed and released and this time saw the flurry of feathers that meant he had made a hit.

The bird had been struck off-centre and was flopping around wildly. Brian jumped on it and grabbed it and slammed it against the ground once, sharply, to kill it. Then he stood and retrieved his arrows and made sure they were all right and went down to the lake to wash the blood off his hands. He kneeled at the water's edge and put the dead bird and his weapons down and dipped his hands into the water.

It was very nearly the last act of his life. Later he would not know why he started to turn – some smell or sound. A tiny brushing sound. But something caught his ear or nose and he began to turn, and had his head half around, when he saw a brown wall of fur detach itself from the forest to his rear and come down on him like a runaway truck. He just had time to see that it was a moose – he knew them from pictures but did not know, could not guess how large they were – when it hit him. It was a cow and she had no horns, but she took him in the left side of the back with her forehead, took him and threw him out into the water and then came after him to finish the job.

He had another half-second to fill his lungs with air and she was on him again, using her head to drive him down into the mud of the bottom. Insane, he thought. Just that, the word, insane. Mud filled his eyes, his ears, the horn boss on the moose drove him deeper and deeper into the bottom muck, and suddenly it was over and he felt alone.

He sputtered to the surface, sucking air and fighting panic, and when he wiped the mud and water out of his eyes and cleared them he saw the cow standing sideways to him, not ten feet away, calmly chewing on a lilypad root. She didn't appear to even see him, or didn't seem to care about him, and Brian turned carefully and began to swim-crawl out of the water.

As soon as he moved, the hair on her back went up and she charged him again, using her head and front hooves this time, slamming him back and down into the water, on his back this time, and he screamed the air out of his lungs and hammered on her head with his fists and filled his throat with water and she left again.

Once more he came to the surface. But he was hurt now, hurt inside, hurt in his ribs and he stayed hunched over, pretending to be dead. She was standing again, eating. Brian studied her out of one eye, looking to the bank with the other, wondering how seriously he was injured, wondering if she would let him go this time.

Insane.

He started to move, ever so slowly; her head turned and her back hair went up – like the hair on an angry dog – and he stopped, took a slow breath, the hair went down and she ate. Move, hair up, stop, hair down, move, hair up – a half-foot at a time until he was at the edge of the water. He stayed on his hands and knees – indeed, was hurt so he wasn't sure he could walk anyway, and she seemed to accept that and let him crawl, slowly, out of the water and up into the trees and brush.

When he was behind a tree he stood carefully and took stock. Legs seemed all right, but his ribs were hurt bad – he could only take short breaths and then he had a jabbing pain – and his right shoulder seemed

119

to be wrenched somehow. Also his bow and spear and foolbird were in the water.

At least he could walk and he had just about decided to leave everything when the cow moved out of the deeper water and left him, as quickly as she'd come, walking down along the shoreline in the shallow water, with her long legs making sucking sounds when she pulled them free of the mud. Hanging on a pine limb, he watched her go, half expecting her to turn and come back to run over him again. But she kept going and when she was well gone from sight he went to the bank and found the bird, then waded out a bit to get his bow and spear. Neither of them were broken and the arrows, incredibly, were still on his belt in the pouch, although messed up with mud and water.

It took him most of an hour to work his way back around the lake. His legs worked well enough, but if he took two or three fast steps he would begin to breathe deeply and the pain from his ribs would stop him and he would have to lean against a tree until he could slow back down to shallow breathing. She had done more damage than he had originally thought, the insane cow – no sense at all to it. Just madness. When he got to the shelter he crawled inside and was grateful that the coals were still glowing and that he had thought to get wood first thing in the mornings to be ready for the day, grateful that he had thought to get enough wood for two or three days at a time, grateful that he had fish nearby if he needed to eat, grateful, finally, as he dozed off, that he was alive.

So insane, he thought, letting sleep cover the pain in his chest – such an insane attack for no reason

120

and he fell asleep with his mind trying to make the moose have reason.

The noise awakened him.

It was a low sound, a low roaring sound that came from wind. His eyes snapped open not because it was loud but because it was new. He had felt wind in his shelter, felt the rain that came with wind and had heard thunder many times in the past forty-seven days but not this, not this noise. Low, almost alive, almost from a throat somehow, the sound, the noise was a roar, a far-off roar but coming at him and when he was fully awake he sat up in the darkness, grimacing with pain from his ribs.

The pain was different now, a tightened pain, and it seemed less – but the sound. So strange, he thought. A mystery sound. A spirit sound. A bad sound. He took some small wood and got the fire going again, felt some little comfort and cheer from the flames but also felt that he should get ready. He did not know how, but he should get ready. The sound was coming for him, was coming just for him, and he had to get ready. The sound wanted him.

He found the spear and bow where they were hanging on the pegs of the shelter wall and brought his weapons to the bed he had made of pine boughs. More comfort, but like the comfort of the flames it didn't work with this new threat that he didn't understand yet.

Restless threat, he thought, and stood out of the shelter away from the flames to study the sky but it was too dark. The sound meant something to him, something from his memory, something he had read

121

about. Something he had seen on television. Something . . . oh, he thought. Oh no.

It was wind, wind like the sound of a train, with the low belly roar of a train. It was a tornado. That was it! The roar of a train meant bad wind and it was coming for him. God, he thought, on top of the moose not this – not this.

But it was too late, too late to do anything. In the strange stillness he looked to the night sky, then turned back into his shelter and was leaning over to go through the door opening when it hit. Later he would think of it and find that it was the same as the moose. Just insanity. He was taken in the back by some mad force and driven into the shelter on his face, slammed down into the pine branches of his bed.

At the same time the wind tore at the fire and sprayed red coals and sparks in a cloud around him. Then it backed out, seemed to hesitate momentarily, and returned with a massive roar; a roar that took his ears and mind and body.

He was whipped against the front wall of the shelter like a rag, felt a ripping pain in his ribs again, then was hammered back down into the sand once more while the wind took the whole wall, his bed, the fire, his tools – all of it – and threw it out into the lake, gone out of sight, gone for ever. He felt a burning on his neck and reached up to find red coals there. He brushed those off, found more on his trousers, brushed those away, and the wind hit again, heavy gusts, tearing gusts. He heard trees snapping in the forest around the rock, felt his body slipping out and clawed at the rocks to hold himself down. He couldn't think, just held and knew that he was praying but didn't know what the prayer was – knew that he wanted to be, stay and be, and then the wind moved to the lake.

Brian heard the great, roaring sucking sounds of water and opened his eyes to see the lake torn by the wind, the water slamming in great waves that went in all ways, fought each other and then rose in a spout of water going up into the night sky like a wet column of light. It was beautiful and terrible at the same time.

The tornado tore one more time at the shore on the opposite side of the lake – Brian could hear trees being ripped down – and then it was done, gone as rapidly as it had come. It left nothing, nothing but Brian in the pitch dark. He could find nothing of where his fire had been, not a spark, nothing of his shelter, tools or bed, even the body of the foolbird was gone. I am back to nothing he thought, trying to find things in the dark – back to where I was when I crashed. Hurt, in the dark, just the same.

As if to emphasise his thoughts the mosquitoes – with the fire gone and protective smoke no longer saving him – came back in thick, nostril-clogging swarms. All that was left was the hatchet at his belt. Still there. But now it began to rain and in the downpour he would never find anything dry enough to get a fire going, and at last he pulled his battered body back in under the overhang, where his bed had been, and wrapped his arms around his ribs.

Sleep didn't come, couldn't come with the insects ripping at him, so he lay the rest of the night, slapping mosquitoes and chewing with his mind on the day. This morning he had been fat – well, almost fat – and happy, sure of everything, with good weapons and food and the sun in his face and things looking good for the future, and within one day, just one day, he had been run over by a moose and a tornado, had lost everything and was back to square one. Just like that.

A flip of some giant coin and he was the loser.

But there is a difference now, he thought – there really is a difference. I might be hit but I'm not done. When the light comes I'll start to rebuild. I still have the hatchet and that's all I had in the first place.

Come on, he thought, baring his teeth in the darkness – come on. Is that the best you can do? Is that all you can hit me with – a moose and a tornado? Well, he thought, holding his ribs and smiling, then spitting mosquitoes out of his mouth. Well, that won't get the job done. That was the difference now. He had changed, and he was tough. I'm tough where it counts – tough in the head.

In the end, right before dawn a kind of cold snap came down – something else new, this cold snap – and the mosquitoes settled back into the damp grass and under the leaves and he could sleep. Or doze. And the last thought he had that morning as he closed his eyes was: I hope the tornado hit the moose.

When he awakened the sun was cooking the inside of his mouth and had dried his tongue to leather. He had fallen into a deeper sleep with his mouth open just at dawn and it tasted as if he had been sucking on his foot all night.

He rolled out and almost bellowed with pain from his ribs. They had tightened in the night and seemed to pull at his chest when he moved. He slowed his

124

movements and stood slowly, without stretching unduly, and went to the lake for a drink. At the shore he kneeled, carefully and with great gentleness, and drank and rinsed his mouth. To his right he saw that the fish pond was still there, although the willow gate was gone and there were no fish. They'll come back, he thought, as soon as I can make a spear or bow and get one or two for bait they'll come back.

He turned to look at his shelter – saw that some of the wood for the wall was scattered around the beach but was still there, then saw his bow jammed into a driftwood log, broken but with the precious string intact. Not so bad now – not so bad. He looked down the shoreline for other parts of his wall and that's when he saw it.

Out in the lake, in the short part of the L, something curved and yellow was sticking six or eight inches out of the water. It was a bright colour, not an earth or natural colour, and for a second he could not place it, then he knew it for what it was.

'It's the tail of the plane.' He said it aloud, half expecting to hear somebody answer him. There it was, sticking up out of the water. The tornado must have flipped the plane around somehow when it hit the lake, changed the position of the plane and raised the tail. Well, he thought. Well, just look at that. And at the same moment a cutting thought hit him. He thought of the pilot, still in the plane, and that brought a shiver and massive sadness that seemed to settle on him like a weight and he thought that he should say or do something for the pilot; some words but he didn't know any of the right words, the religious words.

So he went down to the side of the water and

looked at the plane and focused his mind, the way
he did when he was hunting the foolbirds and wanted
to concentrate, focused it on the pilot and thought:
Have rest. Have rest for ever.

SEVENTEEN

He turned back to his campsite and looked at the wreckage. He had a lot to do, rebuild his shelter, get a new fire going, find some food or get ready to find some food, make weapons – and he had to work slowly because his ribs hurt.

First things first. He tried to find some dry grass and twigs, then peeled bark from a nearby birch to shred into a fire nest. He worked slowly but even so, with his new skill he had a fire going in less than an hour. The flames cut the cool damp morning, crackled and did much to bring his spirits up, not to mention chasing away the incessant mosquitoes. With the fire going he searched for dry wood – the rain had driven water into virtually all the wood he could find – and at last located some in a thick evergreen where the top branches had covered the lower dead ones, keeping them dry.

He had great difficulty breaking them, not being able to pull much with his arm or chest muscles, but finally got enough to keep the fire going all day and into the night. With that he rested a bit, eased his chest, and then set about getting a shelter built.

Much of the wood from his original wall was still nearby and up at the back of the ridge he actually found a major section of the weave still intact. The wind had torn it out, lifted it and thrown it to the top of the ridge and Brian felt lucky once more that

he had not been killed or more seriously injured –
which would have been the same, he thought. If he
couldn't hunt he would die and if he were injured
badly he would not be able to hunt.

He jerked and dragged wood around until the wall
was once more in place – crudely, but he could
improve it later. He had no trouble finding enough
pine boughs to make a new bed. The storm had torn
the forest to pieces – up behind the ridge it looked
as if a giant had become angry and used some kind
of a massive mincer on the trees. Huge pines were
twisted and snapped off, blown sideways. The
ground was so littered, with limbs and tree-tops
sticking every which way, that it was hard to get
through. He pulled enough thick limbs in for a bed,
green and spicy with the new broken sap smell, and
by evening he was exhausted, hungry and hurting,
but he had something close to a place to live in again,
a place to be.

Tomorrow, he thought, as he lay back in the darkness. Tomorrow maybe the fish would be back and
he would make a spear and new bow and get some
food. Tomorrow he would find food and refine the
camp and bring things back to sanity from the one
completely insane day.

He faced the fire. Curving his body, he rested his
head on his arm, and began to sleep when a picture
came into his head. The tail of the plane sticking out
of the water. There it was, the tail sticking up. And
inside the plane, near the tail somewhere, was the
survival pack. It must have survived the crash because
the plane's main body was still intact. That was the
picture – the tail sticking up and the survival pack
inside – right there in his mind as he dozed. His eyes

128

snapped opened. If I could get at the pack, he thought. Oh, if I could get at the pack. It probably had food and knives and matches. It might have a sleeping bag. It might have fishing gear. Oh, it must have so many wonderful things – if I could get at the pack and just get some of those things. I would be rich. So rich if I could get at the pack.

Tomorrow. He watched the flames and smiled. Tomorrow I'll see. All things come tomorrow.

He slept, deep and down with only the picture of the plane tail sticking up in his mind. A healing sleep.

In the morning he rolled out before true light. In the grey dawn he built up the fire and found more wood for the day, feeling almost chipper because his ribs were much better now. With camp ready for the day he looked towards the lake. Part of him half-expected the plane tail to be gone, sunk back into the depths, but he saw that it was still there, didn't seem to have moved at all.

He looked down at his feet and saw that there were some fish in his fish pen looking for the tiny bits of bait still left from before the wind came. He fought impatience to get on the plane project and remembered sense, remembered what he had learned. First food, because food made strength; first food, then thought, then action. There were fish at hand here, and he might not be able to get anything from the plane. That was all a dream.

The fish were real and his stomach, even his new shrunken stomach, was sending signals that it was savagely empty.

He made a fish spear with two points, not peeling the bark all the way back but just working on the

129

pointed end. It took him an hour or so and all the time he worked he sat looking at the tail of the plane sticking up in the air, his hands working on the spear, his mind working on the problem of the plane.

When the spear was done, although still crude, he jammed a wedge between the points to spread them apart and went to the fish pond. There were not clouds of fish but at least ten, and he picked one of the larger ones, a round fish almost six inches long, and put the spear point in the water, held it, then thrust with a flicking motion of his wrist when the fish was just above the point.

The fish was pinned neatly and he took two more with the same ease, then carried all three back up to the fire. He had a fish board now, a piece of wood he had flattened with the hatchet, that leaned up by the fire for cooking fish so he didn't have to hold a stick all the time. He put the three fish on the board, pushed sharpened pegs through their tails into cracks on the cooking board, and propped it next to the reddest part of the coals. In moments the fish were hissing and cooking with the heat and as soon as they were done, or when he could stand the smell no longer, he picked the steaming meat from under the loosened skin and ate it.

The fish did not fill him, did not even come close – fish meat was too light for that. But they gave him strength – he could feel it moving into his arms and legs – and he began to work on the plane project.

While making the spear he had decided that what he would have to do was make a raft and push-paddle the raft to the plane and tie it there for a working base. Somehow he would have to get into the tail, inside the plane – rip or cut his way in – and however he did it he would need an operating base of some kind. A raft.

Which, he found ruefully, was much easier said than done. There were plenty of logs around. The shore was littered with driftwood, new and old, tossed up and scattered by the tornado. And it was a simple matter to find four of them about the same length and pull them together.

Keeping them together was the problem. Without rope or crosspieces and nails the logs just rolled and separated. He tried wedging them together, crossing them over each other – nothing seemed to work. And he needed a stable platform to get the job done. It was becoming frustrating and he had a momentary loss of temper – as he would have done in the past, when he was the other person.

At that point he sat back on the beach and studied the problem again. Sense, he had to use his sense. That's all it took to solve problems – just sense.

It came then. The logs he had selected were smooth and round and had no limbs. What he needed were logs with limbs sticking out, then he could cross the limbs of one log over the limbs of another and 'weave' them together as he had done his wall, the food shelf cover, and the fish gate. He scanned the area above the beach and found four dry treetops that had been broken off by the storm. These had limbs and he dragged them down to his work area at the water's edge and fitted them together.

It took most of the day. The limbs were cluttered and stuck any which way and he would have to cut one to make another fit, then cut one from another log to come back to the first one, then still another from a third log would have to be pulled in.

But at last, in the late afternoon he was done and the raft – which he called Brushpile One for its looks – hung together even as he pulled it into the water off the beach. It floated well, if low in the water, and in the excitement he started for the plane. He could not stand on it, but would have to swim alongside.

He was out to chest depth when he realised he had no way to keep the raft at the plane. He needed some way to tie it in place so he could work from it.

And for a moment he was stymied. He had no rope, only the bowstring and the other cut shoelace in his tennis shoes – which were by now looking close to dead, his toes showing at the tops. Then he remembered his anorak and he found the tattered part he used for an arrow pouch. He tore it into narrow strips and tied them together to make a rope about four feet long. It wasn't strong, he couldn't use it to do a Tarzan and swing from a tree, but it should hold the raft to the plane.

Once more he slid the raft off the beach and out into the water until he was chest deep. He had left his tennis shoes in the shelter and when he felt the sand turn to mud between his toes he kicked off the bottom and began to swim.

Pushing the raft, he figured, was about like trying to push an aircraft carrier. All the branches that stuck down into the water dragged and pulled and the logs themselves fought any forward motion and he hadn't gone twenty feet when he realised that it was going to be much harder than he thought to get the raft to the plane. It barely moved and if he kept going this way he would just about reach the plane at dark. He

132

decided to turn back again, spend the night and start early in the morning, and he pulled the raft once more on to the sand and wipe-scraped it dry with his hand.

Patience. He was better now but impatience still ground at him a bit so he sat at the edge of the fish pond with the new spear and took three more fish, cooked them and ate them, which helped to pass the time until dark. He also dragged in more wood – endless wood – and then relaxed and watched the sun set over the trees behind the ridge. West, he thought. I'm watching the sun set in the west. And that way was north where his father was, and that way east and that way south – and somewhere to the south and east his mother would be. The news would be on the television. He could visualise more easily his mother doing things than his father because he had never been to where his father lived now. He knew everything about how his mother lived. She would have the small television on the kitchen counter on and be watching the news and talking about how awful it was in South Africa or how cute the baby in the commercial looked. Talking and making sounds, cooking sounds.

He jerked his mind back to the lake. There was great beauty here – almost unbelievable beauty. The sun exploded the sky, just blew it up with the setting colour, and that colour came down into the water of the lake, lit the trees. Amazing beauty and he wished he could share it with somebody and say, 'Look there, and over there, and see that . . .'

But even alone it was beautiful and he fed the fire to cut the night chill. There it is again, he thought, that late summer chill to the air, the smell of fall. He went to sleep thinking a kind of reverse question. He did not know if he would ever get out of this, could not see how it might be, but if he did somehow get home and go back to living the way he had lived, would it be just the opposite? Would he be sitting watching television and suddenly think about the sunset up behind the ridge and wonder how the colour looked in the lake?

Sleep.

In the morning the chill was more pronounced and he could see tiny wisps of vapour from his breath. He threw wood on the fire and blew until it flamed, then banked the flames to last and went down to the lake. Perhaps because the air was so cool the water felt warm as he waded in. He made sure the hatchet was still at his belt and the raft still held together, then set out pushing the raft and kick-swimming towards the tail of the plane.

As before, it was very hard going. Once an eddy of breeze came up against him and he seemed to be standing still and by the time he was close enough to the tail to see the rivets in the aluminium he had pushed and kicked for over two hours, was nearly exhausted and wished he had taken some time to get a fish or two and have breakfast. He was also wrinkled as a prune and ready for a break.

The tail looked much larger when he got next to it, with a major part of the vertical stabiliser showing and perhaps half of the elevators. Only a short piece of the top of the fuselage, the plane's body towards the tail, was out of the water, just a curve of aluminium, and at first he could see no place to tie the raft. But he pulled himself along the elevators to the end and there he found a gap that went in up by the hinges where he could feed his rope through.

With the raft secure he climbed on top of it and lay on his back for fifteen minutes, resting and letting the sun warm him. The job, he thought, looked impossible. To have any chance of success he would have to be strong when he started.

Somehow he had to get inside the plane. All openings, even the small rear cargo hatch, were underwater so he couldn't get at them without diving and coming up inside the plane.

Where he would be trapped.

He shuddered at that thought and then remembered what was in the front of the plane, down in the bottom of the lake, still strapped in the seat, the body of the pilot. Sitting there in the water – Brian could see him, the big man with his hair waving in the current, his eyes open . . .

Stop, he thought. Stop now. Stop that thinking. He was nearly at the point of swimming back to shore and forgetting the whole thing. But the image of the survival pack kept him. If he could get it out of the plane, or if he could just get into it and pull something out. A bar of chocolate.

Even that – just a bar of chocolate. It would be worth it.

But how to get at the inside of the plane?

He rolled off the raft and pulled himself around the plane. No openings. Three times he put his face in the water and opened his eyes and looked down. The water was murky, but he could see perhaps six feet and there was no obvious way to get into the plane. He was blocked.

EIGHTEEN

Brian worked around the tail of the plane two more times, pulling himself along on the stabiliser and the elevator, but there simply wasn't a way in.

Stupid, he thought. I was stupid to think I could just come out here and get inside the plane. Nothing is that easy. Not out here, not in this place. Nothing is easy.

He slammed his fist against the body of the plane and to his complete surprise the aluminium covering gave easily under his blow. He hit it again, and once more it bent and gave and he found that even when he didn't strike it but just pushed, it still moved. It was really, he thought, very thin aluminium skin over a kind of skeleton and if it gave that easily he might be able to force his way through . . .

The hatchet. He might be able to cut or hack with the hatchet. He reached to his belt and pulled the hatchet out, picked a place where the aluminium gave to his push and took an experimental swing at it.

The hatchet cut through the aluminium as it if were soft cheese. He couldn't believe it. Three more hacks and he had a triangular hole the size of his hand and he could see four cables that he guessed were the control cables going back to the tail and he hit the skin of the plane with a frenzied series of hacks to make a still larger opening and he was bending a piece of aluminium away from two aluminium braces of some kind when he dropped the hatchet.

It went straight down past his legs. He felt it bump his foot and then go on down, down into the water and for a second he couldn't understand that he had done it. For all this time, all the living and fighting, the hatchet had been everything – he had always worn it. Without the hatchet he had nothing – no fire, no tools, no weapons – he was nothing. The hatchet was, had been him.

And he had dropped it.

'Arrrgghhh!' He yelled it, choked on it, a snarl-cry of rage at his own carelessness. The hole in the plane was still too small to use for anything and now he didn't have a tool.

'That was the kind of thing I would have done before,' he said to the lake, to the sky, to the trees. 'When I came here – I would have done that. Not now. Not now . . .'

Yet he had and he hung on the raft for a moment and felt sorry for himself. For his own stupidity. But as before, the self-pity didn't help and he knew that he had only one course of action.

He had to get the hatchet back. He had to dive and get it back.

But how deep was it? In the deep end of the gym pool at school he had no trouble getting to the bottom and that was, he was pretty sure, about eleven feet.

Here it was impossible to know the exact depth. The front end of the plane, anchored by the weight of the engine, was obviously on the bottom but it came back up at an angle so the water wasn't as deep as the plane was long.

He pulled himself out of the water so his chest could expand, took two deep breaths and swivelled and dived, pulling his arms and kicking off the raft bottom with his feet.

His first thrust took him down a good eight feet but the visibility was only five feet beyond that and he could not see bottom yet. He clawed down six or seven more feet, the pressure pushing in his ears until he held his nose and popped them and just as he ran out of breath and headed back up he thought he saw the bottom – still four feet below his dive.

He exploded out of the surface, bumping his head on the side of the elevator when he came up and took air like a whale, pushing the stale air out until he wheezed, taking new in. He would have to get deeper yet and still have time to search while he was down there.

Stupid, he thought once more, cursing himself – just dumb. He pulled air again and again, pushing his chest out until he could not possibly get any more capacity, then took one more deep lungful, wheeled and dived again.

This time he made an arrow out of his arms and used his legs to push off the bottom of the raft, all he had in his legs, to spring-snap and propel him down. As soon as he felt himself slowing a bit he started raking back with his arms at his sides, like paddles, and thrusting with his legs like a frog and this time he was so successful that he ran his face into the bottom mud.

He shook his head to clear his eyes and looked around. The plane disappeared out and down in front of him. He thought he could see the windows and that made him think again of the pilot sitting inside and he forced his thoughts from it – but he could see no hatchet. Bad air triggers were starting to go off in his brain and he knew he was limited to seconds now but he held for a moment and tried moving out a bit and just as he ran out of air, knew that he was going to have to blow soon, he saw the handle sticking out of the mud. He made one grab, missed, reached again and felt his fingers close on the rubber. He clutched it and in one motion slammed his feet down into the mud and powered himself up. But now his lungs were ready to explode and he had flashes of colour in his brain, explosions of colour, and he would have to take a pull of water, take it into his lungs and just as he opened his mouth to take it in, to pull in all the water in the lake, his head blew out of the surface and into the light.

'Tchaaak!' It was as if a balloon had exploded. Old air blew out of his nose and mouth and he pulled new in again and again. He reached for the side of the raft and hung there, just breathing, until he could think once more – the hatchet clutched and shining in his right hand.

'All right . . . the plane. Still the plane . . .'

He went back to the hole in the fuselage and began to chop and cut again, peeling the aluminium skin off in pieces. It was slow going because he was careful, very careful with the hatchet, but he hacked and pulled until he had opened a hole large enough to pull his head and shoulders in and look down into the water. It was very dark inside the fuselage and he could see nothing – certainly no sign of the survival pack. There were some small pieces and bits of paper floating on the surface inside the plane – dirt from the floor of the plane that had floated up – but nothing substantial.

Well, he thought. Did you expect it to be easy? So easy that way? Just open her up and get the pack – right?

He would have to open it more, much more so he could poke down inside and see what he could find. The survival pack had been a zippered nylon bag, or perhaps canvas of some kind, and he thought it had been red, or was it grey? Well, that didn't matter. It must have been moved when the plane crashed and it might be jammed down under something else.

He started chopping again, cutting the aluminium away in small triangles, putting each one on the raft as he chopped – he could never throw anything away again, he thought – because they might be useful later. Bits of metal, fish arrowheads or lures, maybe. And when he finally finished again he had cleaned away the whole side and top of the fuselage that stuck out of the water, had cut down into the water as far as he could reach and had a hole almost as big as he was, except that it was crossed and cris-scrossed with aluminium – or it might be steel, he couldn't tell – braces and struts and cables. It was an awful tangled mess, but after chopping some braces away there was room for him to wiggle through and get inside.

He held back for a moment uncomfortable with the thought of getting inside the plane. What if the tail settled back to the bottom and he got caught and couldn't get out? It was a horrible thought. But then he reconsidered. The thing had been up now for two days, plus a bit, and he had been hammering and

140

climbing on it and it hadn't gone back down. It seemed pretty solid.

He eeled in through the cables and struts, wiggling and pulling until he was inside the tail with his head clear of the surface of the water and his legs down on the angled floor. When he was ready, he took a deep breath and pushed down along the floor with his legs, feeling for some kind of fabric or cloth – anything – with his bare feet. He touched nothing but the floor plates.

Up, a new breath, then he reached down to struts underwater and pulled himself beneath the water, his legs pushing down and down almost to the backs of the front seats and finally, on the left side of the plane, he thought he felt his foot hit cloth or canvas.

Up for more air, deep breathing, then one more grab at the struts and pushing as hard as he could he jammed his feet down and hit it again, definitely canvas or heavy nylon, and this time when he pushed his foot he thought he felt something inside it; something hard.

It had to be the bag. Driven forward by the crash, it was jammed into the backs of the seats and caught on something. He tried to reach for it and pull but didn't have the air left and went up for more.

Lungs filled in great gulps, he shot down again, pulling on the struts until he was almost there, then wheeling down head first he grabbed at the cloth. It was the survival bag. He pulled and tore at it to loosen it and just as it broke free and his heart leaped to feel it rise he looked up, above the bag. In the light coming through the side window, the pale green light from the water, he saw the pilot's head only it wasn't the pilot's head any longer.

The fish. He'd never really thought of it, but the fish – the fish he had been eating all this time had to eat, too. They had been at the pilot all this time, almost two months, nibbling and chewing and all that remained was the not quite cleaned skull and when he looked up it wobbled loosely.

Too much. Too much. His mind screamed in horror and he slammed back and was sick in the water, sick so that he choked on it and tried to breathe water and could have ended there, ended with the pilot where it almost ended when they first arrived except that his legs jerked. It was instinctive, fear more than anything else, fear of what he had seen. But they jerked and pushed and he was headed up when they jerked and he shot to the surface, still inside the birdcage of struts and cables.

His head slammed into a bracket as he cleared and he reached up to grab it and was free, in the air, hanging up in the tail.

He hung that way for several minutes, choking and heaving and gasping for air, fighting to clear the picture of the pilot from his mind. It went slowly – he knew it would never completely leave – but he looked towards the shore and there were trees and birds, the sun was getting low and golden over his shelter and when he stopped coughing he could hear the gentle sounds of evening, the peace sounds, the bird sounds and the breeze in the trees.

The peace finally came to him and he settled his breathing. He was still a long way from being finished – had a lot of work to do. The bag was floating next to him but he had to get it out of the plane and on to the raft, then back to shore.

He wiggled out through the struts – it seemed

142

harder than when he came in – and pulled the raft around. The bag fought him. It was almost as if it didn't want to leave the plane. He pulled and jerked and still it wouldn't fit and at last he had to change the shape of it, rearranging what was inside by pushing and pulling at the sides until he had narrowed it and made it longer. Even when it finally came it was difficult and he had to pull first at one side, then another, an inch at a time, squeezing it through.

All of this took some time and when he finally got the bag out and tied on top of the raft it was nearly dark, he was bone tired from working in the water all day, chilled deep, and he still had to push the raft to shore.

Many times he thought he would not make it. With the added weight of the bag – which seemed to get heavier by the foot – coupled with the fact that he was getting weaker all the time, the raft seemed barely to move. He kicked and pulled and pushed, taking the shortest way straight back to shore, hanging to rest many times, then surging again and again.

It seemed to take for ever, and when at last his feet hit bottom and he could push against the mud and slide the raft into the shore weeds to bump against the bank he was so weak he couldn't stand, had to crawl; so tired he didn't even notice the mosquitoes that tore into him like a grey, angry cloud.

He had done it.

That's all he could think now. He had done it.

He turned and sat on the bank with his legs in the water and pulled the bag ashore and began the long drag – he couldn't lift it – back down the shoreline to his shelter. Two hours, almost three he dragged and stumbled in the dark, brushing the mosquitoes away, sometimes on his feet, more often on his knees, finally to drop across the bag and to sleep when he made the sand in front of the doorway.

He had done it.

NINETEEN

Treasure.

Unbelievable riches. He could not believe the contents of the survival pack.

The night before he was so numb with exhaustion he couldn't do anything but sleep. All day in the water had tired him so much that, in the end, he had fallen asleep in front of the doorway, oblivious even to the mosquitoes, to the night, to anything. But with false grey dawn he had awakened, instantly, and began to dig in the pack – to find amazing, wonderful things.

There was a sleeping bag – which he hung to dry over his shelter roof on the outside – and foam sleeping pad. An aluminium cooking set with four little pots and two frying pans; it actually even had a fork and knife and spoon. A waterproof container with matches and two small butane lighters. A sheath knife with a compass in the handle. As if a compass would help him, he thought, smiling. A first-aid kit with bandages and tubes of antiseptic paste and small scissors. A cap that said CESSNA across the front in large letters. Why a cap, he wondered. It was adjustable and he put it on immediately. A fishing kit with four coils of line, a dozen small lures, and hooks and sinkers.

Incredible wealth. It was like all the holidays in the world, all the birthdays there were. He sat in the sun by the doorway where he had dropped the night before and pulled the presents – as he thought of them – out one at a time to examine them, turn them in the light, touch them and feel them with his hands and eyes.

Something that at first puzzled him. He pulled out what seemed to be the broken-off, bulky stock of a rifle and he was going to put it aside, thinking it might be for something else in the pack, when he shook it and it rattled. After working at it a moment he found the butt of the stock came off and inside there was a barrel and magazine and action assembly, with a clip and a full box of fifty shells. It was a .22 survival rifle – he had seen one once in the sports shop where he went for bike parts – and the barrel screwed on to the stock. He had never owned a rifle, never fired one, but had seen them on television, of course, and after a few moments figured out how to put it together by screwing the action on to the stock, how to load it and put the clip full of bullets into the action.

It was a strange feeling, holding the rifle. It somehow removed him from everything around him. Without the rifle he had to fit in, to be part of it all, to understand it and use it – the woods, all of it. With the rifle, suddenly, he didn't have to know; did not have to be afraid or understand. He didn't have to get close to a foolbird to kill it – didn't have to know how it would stand if he didn't look at it and moved off to the side.

The rifle changed him, the minute he picked it up, and he wasn't sure he liked the change very much. He set it aside, leaning it carefully against the wall. He could deal with that feeling later. The fire was out

146

and he used a butane lighter and a piece of birchbark with small twigs to get another one started – marvelling at how easy it was but feeling again that the lighter somehow removed him from where he was, what he had to know. With a ready flame he didn't have to know how to make a spark nest, or how to feed the new flames to make them grow. As with the rifle, he wasn't sure he liked the change.

Up and down, he thought. The pack was wonderful but it gave him up and down feelings.

With the fire going and sending up black smoke and a steady roar from a pitch-smelling chunk he put on, he turned once more to the pack. Rummaging through the food packets – he hadn't brought them out yet because he wanted to save them until last, glory in them – he came up with a small electronic device completely encased in a plastic bag. At first he thought it was a radio or cassette player and he had a surge of hope because he missed music, missed sound, missed hearing another voice. But when he opened the plastic and took the thing out and turned it over he could see that it wasn't a receiver at all. There was a coil of wire held together on the side by tape and it sprung into a three foot long antenna when he took the tape off. No speaker, no lights, just a small switch at the top and on the bottom he finally found, in small print: Emergency Transmitter.

That was it. He turned the switch back and forth a few times but nothing happened – he couldn't even hear static – so, as with the rifle, he set it against the wall and went back to the bag. It was probably ruined in the crash, he thought.

Two bars of soap.

He had bathed regularly in the lake, but not with

147

soap and he thought how wonderful it would be to wash his hair. Thick with grime and smoke dirt, frizzed by wind and sun, matted with fish and fool-bird grease, his hair had grown and stuck and tangled and grown until it was a clumped mess on his head. He could use the scissors from the first-aid kit to cut it off, then wash it with soap.

And then, finally – the food.

It was all freeze-dried and in such quantity that he thought, With this I could live for ever. Packet after packet he took out, beef dinner with potatoes, cheese and noodle dinners, chicken dinners, egg and potato breakfasts, fruit mixes, drink mixes, dessert mixes, more dinners and breakfasts than he could count easily, dozens and dozens of them all packed in water-proof bags, all in perfect shape and when he had them all out and laid against the wall in stacks he couldn't stand it and he went through them again.

If I'm careful, he thought, they'll last as long as . . . as long as I need them to last. If I'm careful . . . No. Not yet. I won't be careful just yet. First I am going to have a feast. Right here and now I am going to cook up a feast and eat until I drop and then I'll be careful.

He went into the food packs once more and selected what he wanted for his feast: a four-person beef and potato dinner, with orange drink for an appetiser and something called a peach whip for dessert. Just add water, it said on the packets, and cook for half an hour or so until everything was normal-size and done.

Brian went to the lake and got water in one of the aluminium pots and came back to the fire. Just that amazed him – to be able to carry water to the fire in a pot. Such a simple act and he hadn't been able to do it for almost two months. He guessed at the amounts and put the beef dinner and peach dessert on to boil, then went back to the lake and brought water to mix with the orange drink.

It was sweet and tangy – almost too sweet – but so good that he didn't drink it fast, held it in his mouth and let the taste go over his tongue. Tickling on the sides, sloshing it back and forth and then down, swallow, then another.

That, he thought, that is just fine. Just fine. He got more lake water and mixed another one and drank it fast, then a third one, and he sat with that near the fire but looking out across the lake, thinking how rich the smell was from the cooking beef dinner. There was garlic in it and some other spices and the smells came up to him and made him think of home, his mother cooking, the rich smells of the kitchen, and at that precise instant, with his mind full of home and the smell from the food filling him, the plane appeared.

He had only a moment of warning. There was a tiny drone but as before it didn't register, then suddenly, roaring over his head low from behind the ridge a bushplane with floats fairly exploded into his life.

It passed directly over him, very low, tipped a wing sharply over the tail of the crashed plane in the lake, cut power, glided down the long part of the L of the lake, then turned and glided back, touching the water gently once, twice, and settling with a spray to taxi and stop with its floats gently bumping the beach in front of Brian's shelter.

He had not moved. It had all happened so fast that

he hadn't moved. He sat with the pot of orange drink still in his hand, staring at the plane, not quite understanding it yet; not quite knowing yet that it was over.

The pilot cut the engine, opened the door and got out, balanced and stepped forward on the float to hop on to the sand without getting his feet wet. He was wearing sunglasses and he took them off to stare at Brian.

'I heard your emergency transmitter – then I saw the plane when I came over . . .' He trailed off, cocked his head, studying Brian. 'Damn. You're him, aren't you? You're that kid. They quit looking, a month, no, almost two months ago. You're him, aren't you? You're that kid . . .'

Brian was standing now, but still silent, still holding the drink. His tongue seemed to be stuck to the roof of his mouth and his throat didn't work right. He looked at the pilot, and the plane, and down at himself – dirty and ragged, burned and lean and tough – and he coughed to clear his throat.

'My name is Brian Robeson,' he said. Then he saw that his stew was done, the peach whip almost done, and he waved to it with his hand. 'Would you like something to eat?'

HATCHET:
THE RETURN

To my daughter, Lynn, with love

ONE

Brian opened the door and stood back. There were three men, all in dark suits, standing on the front porch. They were large but not fat, well built, with bodies in decent shape. One of them was slightly thinner than the other two.

'Brian Robeson?'

Brian nodded. 'Yes.'

The thin man smiled and stepped forward and held out his hand. 'I'm Derek Holtzer. These other two are Bill Mannerly and Erik Ballard. Can we come in?'

Brian held the door open to let them come in. 'Mother isn't home right now . . . '

'It's you we want to see.' Derek stopped just in the entry-way and the other two did the same. 'Of course, we'll wish to speak to your mother and father as well, but we came to see you. Didn't you get a call about us?'

Brian shook his head. 'I don't think so. I mean, I know I didn't, but I don't think Mother did either. She would have said something.'

'How about your father?'

'He . . . doesn't live here. My parents are divorced.'

'Oh. Sorry.' Derek truly looked embarrassed. 'I didn't know.'

'It happens.' Brian shrugged, but it was still new enough, just over a year and a half, to feel painful. He mentally pushed it away and had a sudden thought of his

1

own foolishness. Three men he did not know were in the house. They did not look threatening, but you never knew.

'What can I do for you?'

'Well, if you don't know anything about any of this, maybe we should wait for your mother to come home. We can come back.'

Brian nodded. 'Whatever you want . . . but you could tell me what it's about, if you wanted to.'

'Maybe I'd better check on you first. Are you the Brian Robeson who survived alone in the Canadian woods for two months?'

'Fifty-four days,' Brian said. 'Not quite two months. Yes – that's me.'

'Good.'

'Are you from the press?' For months after his return home, Brian had been followed by the press. Even after the television special – a camera crew went back with him to the lake and he showed them how he'd lived – they stayed after him. Newspapers, television, book publishers – they called him at home, followed him to school. It was hard to get away from them. One man even offered him money to put his face on a T-shirt, and a jeans company wanted to come out with a line of Brian Robeson Survival Jeans.

His mother had handled them all, with the help – through the mail – of his father, and he had some money in an account for college. Actually, enough to complete college. But it had finally slowed down and he didn't miss it.

At first it had been exciting, but soon the thrill had worn off. He was famous, and that wasn't too bad, but when they started following him with cameras and wanting to make movies of him and his life it got a little crazy.

He met a girl in school, Deborah McKenzie. They hit it off and went on a few dates, and pretty soon the press was bugging *her* as well and that was too much. He started going out the back door, wearing sunglasses, meeting Deborah in out-of-the-way places, and sliding down the hallways in school. He was only too glad when people stopped noticing him.

And here they were again. 'I mean, are you with television or anything?'

Derek shook his head. 'Nope – not even close. We're with a government survival school.'

'Instructors?'

Derek shook his head. 'Not exactly. Bill and Erik are instructors, but I'm a psychologist. We work with people who may need to survive in bad situations – you know, like downed pilots, astronauts, soldiers. How to live off the land and get out safely.'

'What do you want with me?'

Derek smiled. 'You can probably guess . . . '

Brian shook his head.

'Well, to make it short, we want you to do it again.'

TWO

Brian stared at him. 'It's a joke, right?'

Derek shook his head. 'Not at all – but I think we should wait for your mother to come home and talk to her and your father. We'll come back later.'

He turned to leave and the other two men, still silent, followed him to the door.

'Just a minute.' Brian stopped them. 'Maybe I didn't understand what you said – let me get it straight. You want me to go back and do it over again? Live in the woods with nothing but a hatchet?'

Derek nodded. 'That's it.'

'But that's crazy. It was . . . rough. I mean, I almost died and it was just luck that I made it out.'

Derek shook his head. 'No. Not luck. You had something more going for you besides luck.'

Brian had a mental picture of the porcupine coming into his shelter in the dark, throwing the hatchet and hitting the rock embedded in the wall and getting sparks. If the porcupine hadn't come in and he hadn't thrown the hatchet, and if the hatchet hadn't hit the rock just right, there wouldn't have been sparks and he wouldn't have had a fire and he might not be standing here talking to this man now. 'Most of it was luck . . . '

'Let me explain what I mean.'

Brian waited.

'We teach what you did, or we try to. But the truth is,

4

we have never done it and we don't know anybody who has ever done it. Not for real.' He shrugged, his shoulders moving under the jacket. 'Oh, we do silly little tests, you know, where we go out and pretend to survive. But nobody in our field has ever *had* to do it – where everything is on the line.' He looked directly at Brian. 'Like you.'

The one named Bill Mannerly stepped forward. 'We want you to teach us. Not from a book, not from pamphlets or training films, but really *teach* us what it's like. So we can teach others more accurately.'

Brian smiled. He couldn't help it. 'You mean take a class out and show them what I did?'

Derek held up his hands and shook his head. 'No. Not like that. Nothing phony. We haven't worked it all out yet, but we thought one of us would go with you and stay out there with you, live the way you live, watch you – learn. *Learn.* Take notebooks and make notes, write everything down. We really want to know how you did it – all the parts of it.'

Brian believed him. His voice was soft and sincere and his eyes were honest, but still Brian shook his head. 'It wasn't like you think. It wasn't a camping trip. I lost weight, but more than that, I didn't come back the same.' And, he thought, I'm still not the same; I'll never be the same. He could not walk through a park without watching the trees for game, could not *not* hear things. Sometimes he wanted not to see, not to hear everything around him – noise, colours, movement. But he couldn't blank them out. He saw, heard, smelled everything.

'That's what we want to know. Those things.' Derek smiled. 'Look, don't say no yet. Let us come back and

5

talk to your mother, explain it all, and then you can make a decision. All right?'

Brian nodded slowly. 'All right. Just to talk, right?'

'Just to talk.'

The three men left, and Brian looked at the digital clock on the table in the entryway. It would be an hour before his mother got home. He had some studying to do – it was the end of May and there were finals – but he decided to cook dinner.

He loved to cook.

It was one of the things that had changed about him from the time when he was in the woods. He thought of it as the Time.

Just that. The Time. When he was speaking quietly to Deborah about it – he'd tried to tell her of it, all of it, including the moments when he tried to end himself – when he spoke to her about it, he always started it with just those words:

The Time.

A year had passed, and in the world around him not much had changed. His mother still saw the man, though not as much, and Brian thought it might be passing, what they had between them. The divorce was still final – and would probably remain so. He'd gone to visit his father after the Time and found that he'd fallen in love with another woman and was going to marry her.

Things ground on, a day at a time.

But Brian had changed, completely.

And one of the things that had happened was that now he loved to cook. There was something about the food, preparing the food, looking at the food – there was so *much* of it compared to what he'd had in the woods. He enjoyed taking the food out, working with it and cooking

6

it and serving it and eating it. Chewing each bite, *knowing* the food, watching other people eat. Sometimes he would just sit and watch his mother eat what he had cooked, and once it bothered her so much that she looked up at him, a piece of sauteed beef on a fork halfway to her mouth.

'What is it?'

'I'm just watching you eat,' he'd said to her. 'It's something – eating. Just to see somebody eat. It's really something.'

'Are you . . . all right?' she'd asked. Of course, he wasn't – or maybe he was and had never been all right before in his life. But he'd smiled and nodded.

'Sure, fine . . . '

But it was more that he couldn't tell her what was wrong, or even if anything was wrong – he couldn't really talk to anybody about it because nobody understood what he meant.

His father and mother had insisted that he go to a counsellor when he first came back, and more to humour them than anything else he went, but it didn't help. The counsellor thought he was somehow mentally injured, somehow harmed, and the truth was almost the exact opposite. He tried to tell the counsellor that he was more than he had been, not less – not just older, not just fifteen when before he had been fourteen, but more. Much more. But the counsellor didn't understand, couldn't understand, because he hadn't been with Brian in the woods during the time. The Time.

'I discovered fire,' Brian told the counsellor.

'Well, sure, but you're back now — '

Brian had stopped him. 'No. You don't understand. I truly *discovered* fire – the way some man or woman did

7

it thousands and thousands of years ago. I discovered fire where it had been hidden in the rock for all of time and it was there for me. It doesn't matter that we have matches or lighters or that fire is easy to make here in the other part of the world. I truly and honestly discovered fire. It was a great thing, a very great thing . . . '

The counsellor had sat behind his desk and smiled and nodded and tried to know what Brian was speaking about, but it wasn't there – he couldn't.

And that became the way of it for Brian. In all his dealings with the new world around him since he was reborn in the woods – as he thought of it – he had to be evasive, hold back. If he told the truth, nobody believed him; and if he was silent – which he found himself becoming more and more – they thought he was sick.

He couldn't win.

He took two pork chops out of the freezer and thawed them in the microwave. Then he found the cookbook and flipped to the page for breaded pork chops.

When he first returned home, he found himself wanting to eat a great deal. He would buy a hamburger, eat it, drink a malt, then think immediately of buying another one, but that only lasted a brief time. His stomach had shrunk and the food made him feel heavy, wrong somehow, and he'd stopped overeating.

But he still took great pleasure in food, and he now prepared the pork chops slowly, enjoying himself as he worked.

He cut the fat off them, breaded them, preheated the oven, and put them in a glass pan. While they were baking he looked at the clock again – his mother was due in less than half an hour and she was never late – and put two

8

potatoes on a plate to bake in the microwave. He would start them when she came home – they baked in a few minutes – and they could eat before the men came back.

THREE

'It was a wonderful meal,' his mother said, leaning back from the table and smiling, 'as usual.'

Brian nodded. 'Something I whipped up.'

They cleared the table. They had become strangely closer since his return. So much of the divorce, and the other man, had bothered him, but coming close to death in the woods had led him to understand some things about himself and other people. He realised that he was not always right, was, indeed, often not right, and at the same time he found that others were not always wrong.

He learned to accept things – his mother, the situation, his life, all of it – and with the acceptance, he found that he admired her.

She was trying to make a go of it alone, working in a real estate office selling lots, and it was rough.

'We have to tàlk,' he said, putting the dishes in the dishwasher. *To have dishes, he thought, just to have dishes and pots and pans and a stove to cook the food – it still marvelled him.* 'Some men are coming over to talk to you.'

'What men?'

He explained Derek and the other two, what they wanted.

'You mean what they *said* they wanted. They might be anybody. We should call the police.'

He shrugged. 'If you want. I was a little worried at

10

first, but they didn't do anything and they seemed all right, so I told them to come back.'

She thought it over and finally nodded. 'Let's see if they come – we'll play it the way it looks best.'

As if on cue the doorbell rang, and she went to the door with Brian following.

Derek stood alone on the front step. He backed away so they could see him well through the peephole in the door.

She opened the door.

'Hello. I'm Derek Holtzer – '

'My son told me about you. Weren't there two others?'

'We thought one man might be less pushy. They stayed in the hotel.'

'Please come in. We'll have some coffee.'

Derek followed her in and they sat down at the dining room table and Derek explained to Brian's mother what he wanted – all that he had told Brian.

'We would control the operation closely,' he said, 'and take every precaution possible. Of course, we wouldn't do anything without your permission, and Brian's father's as well,' Derek concluded.

His mother sipped coffee and put the cup down carefully. Her voice was even, as if talking about the weather. 'I think it's insane.'

Brian half agreed with her. In all the time since his return, he had had dozens of kids and not a few adults say how much they would have liked to do it – be marooned in the woods with nothing but a hatchet. But they always said it when they weren't over a block and a half from a grocery store, usually in a room with lights and cushions on a couch and running water. None of them had ever said it while they were sitting in the dark with mosquitoes

11

plugging their nostrils or night sounds so loud around them they couldn't think.

To want to go back was insane.

And yet.

And yet . . .

Yet there was this small feeling, a tingle at the back of his neck as his hairs went up.

'I know it sounds strange, but Brian has had a unique experience,' Derek said. He set his cup down carefully on the saucer. 'It could save lives if he would help us.'

'It's still insane.' Brian's mother shook her head. 'I don't think you have the slightest idea of what you're asking. You must realise that for the time Brian was gone we thought he was dead. Dead. We were told by experts that he couldn't possibly still be alive and then we got him back. Back from the dead. And now you're asking me – his mother – to send him back out there?'

Derek took a breath, held it, let it out. 'Don't you see? That's exactly *why* we must do it. Because he was thought to be dead and lived, because he did something nobody else could do and if he could share that with us, show us, take us through it with him – he could save others who are in the same place. It's not just what he learned about survival – we know most of that. Or at least the survival instructors do. It's his thinking, his psychological processes, how his mind worked for him – that's what's so important.'

'I have to do it.' God, Brian thought – was that *my* voice?

Both of them looked at Brian. Derek in surprise, his mother with a stunned look on her face.

'What?'

Brian leaned back. 'I know, Mother. But he's right.

12

I . . . learned something there. About how to live – I mean how to *live*. And if it could help others, I have to do it.'

'There is money,' Derek said. 'We can contract him and the government will pay well for his help.'

His mother was still staring at him, but he knew, Brian knew, that she understood. There was much between them since he came back, much understanding. She treated him much more as an adult and she understood. Still, she held back, and the worry was alive in her face. 'Are you sure – absolutely certain?'

Brian sighed. 'I have to – if it will help others.'

She nodded slowly, biting her lower lip. But she nodded.

'I'll have to call his father,' she said. 'He may say no.'

But Brian knew.

He was going.

FOUR

It was strangely easy for him to get in the bush plane. Brian had thought at one time that he would never get in a small plane again, and when he went to visit his father after the Time it had been hard to enter the plane. But now he clambered in and took the seat in back with a relaxed attitude – it all felt the same and yet different somehow.

Derek got in the front and sat next to the pilot and turned to Brian.

'Are you uncomfortable flying?'

Brian shook his head. He looked out the window at his mother standing by the station wagon. They were at a different small airport, but it was the same station wagon with the phony brown wood sides. She waved when she saw him turn to look, and he waved and mouthed 'goodbye' so she could see it.

The pilot started the engine and Brian jumped a little with the noise, but he settled back down, at once.

He still could not quite believe that he was doing it, felt as if he were half in a dream. It had been two weeks since Derek first came to him, and in that time they had made detailed plans. After Brian had further convinced his mother and worked on his father over the phone, Derek had come back with maps and plans and they had included Brian's mother in the whole process.

Derek had decided he should be the one to go – even

though he had little or no survival knowledge – because he was a psychologist and that was the aspect they wished to learn about.

They picked a lake in the middle of the wilderness, perhaps a hundred miles east of the lake Brian had crashed into the first time. Brian's mother thought of using the same lake, but Derek vetoed it because they wanted it all to be new to Brian. The lake was not named on the map, though it fed a river that went south and east until it disappeared off the map.

'We selected the lake carefully,' Derek said, circling it with a felt-tip pen while they sat in Brian's dining room. 'It has the same kind of terrain as the lake you crashed into, and roughly the same altitude and kind of forest.'

'How far is it from help?' Brian's mother asked.

Derek smiled. 'We'll have a radio, and if any trouble develops we can have a plane there in three or four hours. Please don't worry.'

'But I do worry, that's just it.'

She did worry, Brian thought, watching her as the plane taxied out to the runway. She did worry. Again he watched her get smaller and smaller and again he flinched with the noise of the engine throttling up and again he was amazed at how easy the plane slid into the air and flew.

And he was suddenly afraid.

He couldn't help it. His breath quickened and he looked up front at the pilot and thought, here it is again: one pilot and one engine and if either of them quit they were going down. If the pilot died, if he died and Derek couldn't fly, there would be nobody up front to control the plane. Brian would have to lunge over him and grab the wheel, try to get his feet to the rudder pedals . .

15

He shook his head. Easy now, easy and easy and easy. Breathe deeply, fight it. Memories of the crash came sweeping back into his mind. Mental pictures of the plane crashing down through the trees and into the water – the blue-green water, with the dead pilot next to him – suddenly filled his thoughts.

He pulled a long breath, held it, and fought the pictures away. After he'd returned home there had been dreams. Even after he had flown again, going to visit his father, there had been dreams. Not nightmares so much as reliving dreams of the crash and his time in the woods.

The Time.

But now it was different, all different. He looked at the pilot and saw that he was much younger than Jake had been – so young that he had a cassette recorder held with duct tape to the dashboard of the plane and was listening to rock music with a small set of headsets, his chin bobbing with the music. He flew loosely, slouched in the seat, his fingers lightly on the wheel, and something about him, the way he sat and moved with the music, relaxed Brian.

He eased back in the seat and looked out the window. Down and to the right he saw the amphibious float with the wheels on the side. They would land right on the lake, but the pilot could also take off from solid ground.

The floats didn't seem to slow the plane very much, as big as they were, and they skimmed over the trees until the pilot gained enough altitude to make them seem to slow down.

Derek was silent, looking out the side window, and Brian realised it was the first time the man had been silent for as long as he'd known and been with him. He had asked endless questions of Brian.

He'd read all the stories about Brian's 'adventure' (as he put it), had all the news stories on tape, and seemed to have memorised everything that happened to Brian.

'When you ate the chokecherries,' he would say, 'how long did it take you to get sick?'

Or, 'Did you notice any changes in the way you went to the bathroom?'

'Oh, come on,' Brian had said.

'No, really. All these things are important. They could save lives.' And his face would get serious. 'This is really, really important.'

Brian realised then that Derek truly cared. Until that moment, sitting in the dining room at his house with maps all over the table – until that moment Brian wasn't sure he was still going. He had said he would, thought he would, but he wasn't totally certain until he'd looked at Derek's face and realised that Derek really wanted to help people by learning what Brian knew.

So, here he was, in a bush plane heading north. And it somehow seemed perfectly logical, perfectly all right. As if going back were the most normal thing in the world.

He looked out the window, down past the float on the right. They had been flying half an hour and they were already getting over forest. There were still some farms here and there, but less and less of them, even as he watched. When he looked ahead of the plane, through the whirling propeller, he saw the endless trees stretching away to the horizon.

With the fear gone, or controlled, something about the forest drew him; and that was a surprise as well.

His thinking had changed during the time he was at the lake. It had to, or he would have died. He had to revert, to become part of the woods, an animal. But when he

17

came back, and had been back a time, he started to 'rectify,' as he thought of it. He became used to the city again. The first time he went to a mall he became ill, dizzy with all the movement and noise, and to make himself normal again he went back to the mall again and again until finally it didn't bother him.

And the woods slipped away. The dreams came less and less and he began not to think about them. He didn't forget them – he knew he would never forget them – but he didn't think about them as much; and when he did, there wasn't any fondness.

He remembered the rough parts.

The mosquitoes. Tearing at him, clouds of them, the awful, ripping, thick masses of the small monsters trying to bleed him dry.

'What was it like?' His mother had asked him one day when they were sitting in the kitchen. 'What was the main problem – the worst part of it?'

And he thought at first of mosquitoes, started to tell her about them and shook his head.

'Hunger.'

'Really?' She had seemed surprised. 'I thought it would be the danger, or being alone, or the weather.'

'I don't mean hunger like you're thinking of it,' he had told her. 'Not just when you miss a meal and feel like eating a little bit. Or even if you go a day without eating. I mean where you don't think you're ever going to eat again – don't know if there will ever be more food. An end to food. Where you won't eat and you won't eat and then you still won't eat and finally you *still* won't eat and even when you die and are gone, even then there won't be any food. *That* kind of hunger.'

The outburst had made his mother sit back and blink,

18

but he meant it. The hunger was the worst, worse than the mosquitoes, worse than any of it.

Hunger.

He looked out the window again. Only forest below now, forest and lakes and the plane droning. The air was rough, rougher than he remembered from before, but he didn't mind the jolting.

They had left the runway in northern New York in the early morning, but climbing had brought them into the bright sun and it warmed the inside of the plane until it was hot.

Brian was wearing a T-shirt and a baseball cap with a picture of a fish on the front. He pulled the brim down and turned away from the sun. As he turned he saw the equipment in back of the seats.

There was enough for a small army, and it bothered him and he couldn't pin it down – how or why it bothered him.

It just felt wrong.

Derek had gone over the list with his mother. Food for weeks, tent, a rubber boat, first-aid kit and mosquito repellent, fishing gear, a gun – a gun. Just what we need.

'Just for emergencies,' Derek had explained. 'In case we need them – we have everything we need.'

And there it was, he thought. They had everything they needed and it ruined it all, made the whole trip worthless. It wouldn't be the same.

He tapped Derek on the shoulder and the big man turned in his seat.

'Too much,' Brian yelled over the noise of the engine.

'What?'

'Too much stuff.' Brian pointed over his shoulder at the mound of gear.

But Derek misunderstood and nodded and smiled. 'Great, isn't it? We have everything but the kitchen sink.'

Brian shrugged. 'Yeah. Great.'

But it ate at him. What they were going to do proved nothing. They were playing a game and it struck him that Derek did that – his whole life was that. He knew it was unfair to think of the man that way – he didn't, after all, know him very well. But he acted that way. Like it was all a game and Derek was approaching this whole business that way. Just a game. Football. Soccer.

If it didn't work right, they could call time out and eat a good meal and go swimming and sail off into the sunset in the rubber boat shooting things with the gun and talking to people on the radio.

Survival.

Right.

The plane seemed to hang in the sky over the woods, the trees green like a carpet out and out, and Brian sat there and watched them without seeing them and thought that it was wrong.

There was too much.

It was all wrong.

FIVE

He slept.

He couldn't believe it, but he slept. The sound of the plane's engine and the warm sun and the sameness of the green forest all combined to hit him like a hammer, and his face went against the window and he slept.

The sound of the plane engine changing sound – decreasing in pitch – awakened him, and he was embarrassed to see that he had drooled in his sleep.

He wiped his chin.

They were going down.

Brian felt himself stiffen when the plane nosed down. He couldn't help it. But the descent was gradual and controlled and even. When they were still well above the forest, the pilot slowed the plane still further and dropped the flaps. The plane almost seemed to stop in the air, floated on down toward the lake below and to the front, and Brian remembered the last time he'd 'landed' on a lake in a bush plane.

If he'd known about flaps or how to use them, he wouldn't have been going half the speed when he hit the water. With a gentle landing he might have had time to help the pilot, get the survival pack out. He watched the pilot carefully, noted everything he did, and realised how lucky he'd been. The pilot flared the plane out so that when it came down to the lake it seemed to be barely moving. He worked the wheel and rudder pedals to make

21

it float down slowly and easily. Brian had more or less arrowed the plane into the water – through the trees and down – and it was a miracle that he hadn't been killed.

The answer to his problem had come to him while he slept.

It was simple.

The pilot was all business now, his hands working the controls, easing the throttle, settling the plane the last bit down to the lake.

But Derek turned and smiled at Brian. 'Pretty, isn't it?'

And the lake *was* pretty. It was almost perfectly round, pushing out toward an egg shape slightly, but only slightly.

At the bottom edge of the lake and off to the right a short distance a river flowed south and east, and it was amazing to Brian how accurate the map had been.

They had gone over it on the dining room table, showing his mother where they would be, but looking down on it now, it seemed to be almost a model made of the map. The blue of the lake matched the blue of the water on the map and the river cutting southeast through the green forest looked just as it had on the map – delicate, winding.

Derek said something to the pilot – Brian couldn't hear over the sound of the engine – and the pilot nodded and banked the plane to the right, more toward the river, and put it softly on to the lake.

There was absolutely no wind, and the water was as smooth as a mirror. Brian watched out of his window as the float came down, saw its reflection in the water, closer, closer until it touched itself and skimmed across the flatness, settling more and more until the plane slowed nearly to a stop.

22

The pilot headed the plane toward a clearing to the right of where the river left the lake, nudging the throttle now and then to keep it moving on the floats until it at last slid through some green reeds and bumped the shoreline.

He cut the engine.

'We're here,' Derek said, his voice loud in the sudden silence. 'Let's get unloaded.'

He turned and Brian could see that he was excited.

Like a kid, he thought. He's as excited as a kid. *I'm* the kid here, and I'm not excited. That's because he doesn't know. I know and he doesn't.

Derek climbed out on to the float – moving a little stiffly and Brian noted that he wasn't very athletic, seemed not to be too coordinated – and stepped ashore.

The pilot stayed in his seat and Brian moved the passenger seat forward and clambered out of the plane, stepped on the float and then to the dry grass.

Neat, he thought, neat and clean. The thought came into his mind that it was a beautiful day. The sun was out, there were small popcorn clouds moving across the sky, it was a soft summer afternoon.

Then, instantly – in just that part of a second – he changed. Completely. He became, suddenly, what he'd been before at the lake. Part of it, all of it; inside all of it so that every . . . single . . . little . . . *thing* became important.

He didn't just hear birds singing, not just a background sound of birds, but each bird. He listened to each bird. Located it, knew where it was by the sound, listened for the sound of alarm. He didn't just see clouds, but light clouds, scout clouds that came before the heavier clouds that could mean rain and maybe wind. The clouds were coming out of the northwest, and that meant that weather would come with them. Not could, but would. There would be rain. Tonight, late, there would be rain.

His eyes swept the clearing, then up the edge of the clearing, and in those two sweeps he knew – he *knew* the clearing and the woods. There was a stump there that probably held grubs; hardwood there for a bow, and willows there for arrows; a game trail, probably deer, moving off to the left meant other things, porcupines, raccoons, bear, wolves, moose, skunk would be moving on the trail and into the clearing. He flared his nostrils, smelled the air, pulled the air along the sides of his tongue in a hissing sound and tasted it, but there was nothing. Just summer smells. The tang of pines, soft air, some mustiness from rotting vegetation. No animals. At least, nothing fresh.

Derek had seen the change, was staring at him. 'What happened?'

Brian shook his head. 'Nothing.'

'Yes – something did. You changed. Completely. You're not the same person.'

Brian shrugged. 'I was just . . . looking at things. Seeing them.'

'Tell me,' Derek said. He took a notebook out of his pocket. 'Tell me everything you saw.'

'Right now?'

'Yes.'

'Shouldn't we let the pilot go first?'

Derek turned as if seeing the plane for the first time. 'Oh, yes. I almost forgot. He has to get back. Let's unload, and then he can go and you can tell me — '

'No.'

'What?'

24

Brian had made the decision just as he dozed off in the plane and it had settled into his mind while he slept. He knew it was the right thing to do. 'We're not going to unload.'

'What are you talking about?'

Brian looked at the lake, the clearing, the clouds. Seven, eight hours to rain. 'I mean, if we unload all that gear – everything but the kitchen sink, like you said – this whole business will be ruined, wasted.'

'I don't see what you mean – what happens if we have trouble?'

Brian nodded. 'That's it exactly. We *have* trouble. That's what this is all about. You want to learn, but if you have all that backup, it's just more games. It's not real. You wouldn't have that if the situation were real, would you?'

'But we don't have to use it. We don't have to use any of it.'

Brian smiled – a small, almost sad smile. 'I promise you, absolutely promise you, that if that stuff is here you will use it and I will use it. By the third day, when the hunger really starts to work and the mosquitoes keep coming and coming and there isn't any food or a tent and we know it's just there, just in the bag – I guarantee you we will use it. We won't be able *not* to use it.'

So much talk, Brian thought. Just jabber, jabber all the time. Like bluejays. We stand here and talk, and in seven, eight hours it will rain and we don't have shelter or dry wood or a fire going. Talk. 'Leave it all in the plane. Leave it or I'm flying out of here right now. I know what's coming and I don't want to waste it.'

'But we told your mother . . . '

25

Brian hesitated, then sighed. 'I know. But the rule still holds. If we unload, I'm going home. Period. I'll take responsibility.'

Derek studied him. 'You mean it.'

'Absolutely.'

'How about a compromise?'

'What do you mean?'

'We keep the radio in case there's trouble – serious trouble. Then at least we can call for help.'

Brian rubbed his neck, thinking. It wouldn't be the same. Even the radio would taint it. Still, he *had* told his mother not to worry and if he insisted on not using the radio, absolutely not using it . . .

'All right.'

Derek nodded and stepped past him, balanced along the float and reached into the plane. He said something to the pilot, who nodded and looked at Brian through the windshield with a strange look, a studying look. Then he smiled and waved through the plastic and Brian nodded and waved in return.

Derek came back ashore with the radio – a small unit with a weatherproof seal and fresh nicad batteries. He also carried a small plastic briefcase.

'For my papers,' he said. 'I have to take notes, write things down.'

Brian nodded, smiling inside. Derek sounded almost like Brian sounded when he was speaking to his mother or father and wanted to do something. Pleading. *For my papers* . . .

It was a strange feeling for Brian, the role reversal with an adult. He was in charge of an adult and he supposed in this situation it was the best way. But he was

26

uncomfortable with it, the business of being in control over an adult – or anybody, for that matter.

The plane had to be turned. It was nosed into the reeds and the pilot opened the window and asked them to aim the plane around so it could taxi out and take off.

Derek and Brian worked it back and around, wading in the water, pushing at the floats – the water felt warm to Brian, shore warm – and when they had it aimed well out, the pilot started the engine.

He taxied away without looking back and as soon as he was clear of the reeds he gunned the engine, increasing speed until the plane was roaring across the lake.

It bounced once, then again, and was airborne, climbed well over the trees at the end of the lake, circled and came back over them, the pilot wagging the wings as they watched, and then it was gone.

Gone.

'Well,' Derek said. 'Here we are. Alone.'

Brian nodded. He felt a strange loss at watching the plane leave. An emptiness.

'What's next?' Derek asked. 'How do we get the ball in play?'

Brian looked at him. A game, it's all a game. 'A fire. We need a fire and shelter. Soon.'

Derek looked at him, a question in his eyes.

Brian looked at the sky. 'It's warm afternoon now, but with evening the mosquitoes will come and we need smoke to keep them away until coolness in the morning. And we need shelter because it's going to rain in about six and a half hours.'

'Six and a half hours?'

'Sure. Can't you smell it?'

Derek took a breath through his nose, shook his head. 'Nope. Not a thing.'

'You will,' Brian said. 'You will. Now, let's get the ball rolling.' And he set off looking for a fire stone.

SIX

That first night Brian decided he was insane to have come back, insane to have agreed to do it, and insane for sending the plane away with all that wonderful equipment.

Especially the tent.

Brian had allowed them to have almost no survival gear. He decided that not all people put in this position would have a hatchet, so even that old friend was left at home.

He and Derek each had a knife, the kind that folds like a pocketknife, but is bigger and is worn on the belt in a leather case.

Other than that they had what was in their pockets.

Some change, a few dollars in paper money. Derek had a large nail clipper and some credit cards, Brian had pictures of his mother and Deborah in his wallet.

'That's it?' Derek had said early in the evening, while the sun was still on them but low in the west, past the tops of the trees at the edge of the clearing.

'That's it.' Brian had nodded.

'It's not much, is it?'

Brian had said nothing. The truth was, it *wasn't* much – especially for two people. They would need twice as much of everything. Twice as much food, a larger shelter – it changed things.

29

All Brian had needed to worry about before, during the Time, was himself. And that had been bad enough.

The thought of the second person, especially one as green as Derek, had not somehow hit him until just then, in late afternoon.

And then it didn't matter.

The plane was gone.

Things began to disintegrate fast after that.

It was one thing, Brian knew, to have a plan, to want to do things. It was something else to actually get them done.

Brian could not find a fire stone, so there was no fire.

Without fire there could be no smoke, and without smoke they had no protection against the mosquitoes.

They came with first dark and they were as bad as Brian had remembered. Thick clouds of them, whining, filling their eyes and ears and nostrils.

They had made a crude lean-to – Brian missed the overhanging rock with his shelter back inside a great deal. Clearly it would not stop the rain, though they had tried to make rough shingles of old pieces of half-rotted bark, yet it was a start.

But for some reason – some protective thought – they had crawled back into the lean-to when the mosquitoes first came.

As if, Brian thought, they could hide from the little monsters.

'God,' Derek said in a whisper, a tight sound in the darkness back in the lean-to. 'This is insane.'

They were sitting with their jackets pulled over their heads, but due to Derek's size, when he pulled the jacket up, it pulled his shirt up from his waist and exposed a bit of skin there, and when the mosquitoes found that, he pulled the shirt down and it exposed his neck, and when he hunched to cover that, they could get his waist again, and in a small time he was jerking up and down like a yo-yo.

'You must settle,' Brian told him. 'In your mind. There are some fights you can't win, and I think this must be one of them. It will get worse and worse until after the middle of the night, when the coolness comes and the mosquitoes will stop. Or at least a lot of them will.'

And just the words had helped, had calmed Derek and himself as well.

Dozing, listening to the whine of them around his head in the dark as they tried to find a way through the jacket, he thought, *it was the way*. It was the way of things here. The mosquitoes and the night and the coolness that he knew was coming were just the way of it – part of being here – and he thought he should tell Derek, but decided to keep his mouth shut.

Derek would find it for himself. Or he would not, just as Brian had found things out for himself.

Brian left the lean-to and went back outside. There might be part of a breeze later as the rain came and it would help.

There was a sliver of moon, which made enough light to see the lake well, the flat water with the beam of moonlight coming across it, and even with the mosquitoes still working at him he was amazed at the beauty.

There were night sounds – birds, flittering things he knew were bats. He also knew they were eating mosquitoes – he'd read about them in biology – and he thought, *get some, bats. Get some. Get all the mosquitoes there are.*

Something swam into the moonlight on the surface of

31

the lake – either a muskrat or a beaver – and cut a *V* right up the path of the moon, seemed to be heading for the moon, into the moon itself.

Water made sound and he realised it was the river gurgling as it left the lake to his right. Not fast, and not wide – perhaps forty or fifty feet across – the river still seemed to possess force, strength as it ran.

Somehow the beauty overrode the mosquitoes. Brian was standing there, looking through the gap in his jacket – which was still pulled up over his head – when he heard Derek come up alongside him.

'It's incredible, isn't it?' Derek saw it as well, the beauty, and Brian was glad that he could see it, see not just the bad parts but the good as well.

'I had forgotten,' Brian said. 'I had dreams after I got out last time. Not all nightmares, but dreams. I would dream of this, of how pretty it was, how it could stop your breath with it, and then I would wake up in my room with the traffic sounds and the streetlights outside and I would feel bad – miss it. I would miss this.'

'Except for the mosquitoes.'

Brian smiled. 'Well, yes, except for those.'

But even as they talked, the night temperature started to drop and it was as if a switch went off. There were still some mosquitoes, but most of them left and the two of them were left standing in the moonlight.

'Incredible,' Derek said. 'They're just gone.'

'Haven't you run into them before? You know, when you're doing the courses, and all that, for the government?'

Derek nodded. 'Of course. Sort of. I haven't run the courses that much – just once to try to see what it was like and I pretty much failed it. They always have tents and repellent and gear with them. You know, to take the edge off.' He laughed softly. 'I'll change that the next time we have a meeting. It was wrong. Psychologically wrong. You were right to leave all that in the plane – absolutely right.'

Later, when everything changed and he did not think there was hope, that statement was all that kept Brian going.

SEVEN

The rain came about eleven.

Derek had time for one quick joke.

'You said it would be six and a half hours – it's almost seven.'

Then it hit them and there was nothing but water. The clouds had come quickly, covering the stars and moon in what seemed like minutes and then just opened up and dropped everything on them.

'It wasn't just a rain. It was a roaring, ripping downpour of water that almost drove them into the ground.

They had moved back into the lean-to to try to get some rest since the mosquitoes partially lessened, but the temporary roof did nothing, absolutely nothing, to slow the water.

They were immediately soaked, then more soaked, sloppy with water.

They tried moving beneath some overhanging thick willows and birch near the edge of the lake, but the trees also did nothing to slow the downpour and finally they just sat, huddled beneath the willows, and took it.

I have, Brian thought, always been wet.

Always.

Even my soul is wet.

He felt the water running down his back. He judged it to be about the same rate as the faucet in his kitchen sink at home and that made him think of his mother.

Sitting at the table, the dining room table.

With a roof. He'd forgotten how nice a roof could be.

'This is crazy,' he said aloud to Derek next to him, but the rain took the words away and he leaned against a birch and closed his eyes and, finally, took it.

I'm here, he thought, *to show Derek how I did it, how this can be done, for other people, and right now there is nothing to do but take it.*

And somehow the night passed.

Close to dawn the rain stopped and there was a softness after the rain, almost a warmth, and that brought the mosquitoes back for one more run. By the time the sun came up, full up over the lake and brought them warmth, Brian felt like he'd been hit by a truck while playing in a puddle.

He ached all over, and when he turned to see Derek – leaned back against a tree sideways, curled into a ball with his jacket still over his head – Brian laughed.

The sound awakened Derek, who was not really asleep, and he looked out of the jacket. 'What's so funny?'

Brian shook his head. 'I guess it's not funny, but you look so miserable—'

'You ought to see yourself.' Derek grinned. 'Kind of like a drowned rat.'

'That's about how I feel.'

They stood, and Brian moved down to the shore of the lake. He stripped his clothes down to his shorts and wrung them out and hung them on some branches to dry.

This day, he thought, *this day we must find shelter and a fire stone and get a fire going and some food.*

Hunger was already there.

Not the kind that would come later, the cutting kind he remembered so well and that still made his mouth

35

water when he walked past a grocery store or fast-food place.

But it was there.

'We have a problem,' Derek said suddenly. He had moved down to the lake shore as well and had stripped down to hang his clothes to dry.

'That's for sure,' Brian said. 'We've definitely got a problem.'

'No. Not what we're doing here. I mean, we have a problem with you.'

'What do you mean?'

'You're so . . . so quiet. I mean, I see you looking at things and thinking, but I don't know what you're thinking about or what you're working out. I have to know all this to write about it, to tell people what to do.'

Brian nodded. 'I understand. It's just that the last time I did this I was alone.'

I would have killed, Brian thought suddenly, for someone to talk to, someone to share it with, someone to hear me; and now that I have someone, I don't talk.

'It's kind of strange having someone here with me.'

Derek nodded. 'That's what I mean. You have to tell me everything, externalise it all for me, so I can write it.'

Derek moved back to the lean-to, where he'd left the radio and his weatherproof briefcase. Inside the briefcase he had notebooks, each one in a plastic bag, and he took one out now with a pencil and began to write carefully. When he'd written something he looked up at Brian, waiting. 'All right. I'm ready.'

Externalise, Brian thought. How do you externalise?

'Well, I'm thinking now that we should make sure we get a shelter today and then get a fire today and get some food today . . . '

36

I sound like a catalogue, he thought, *like I'm reading a telephone book*.

But Derek nodded and started writing and Brian thought of what he really wanted to say.

We should grab the radio and call for the plane and go home and eat a hamburger and a malt, maybe eight or ten Cokes, a steak, some roasts and pork chops . . .

He shook his head.

'There,' Derek said. 'What were you thinking there?'

Brian stared at him, then shook his head. 'You don't want to know. Just junk.'

He walked away into the day. It was enough. Enough of talk. Enough of externalising. Another night like last night would kill him.

He left his clothes to dry, but wore his tennis shoes and noticed that Derek did the same thing – although he carried the notebook as well – and Brian set off along the lakeshore to the left.

Rule one, he thought, don't leave the lakeshore or you'll get lost. Then he remembered Derek and said it aloud.

'Thank you,' Derek said, rather properly. Standing in his underwear holding the notebook he looked like somebody out of an old, funny movie and Brian had trouble keeping a straight face. 'That's exactly what I meant by externalising.'

'We're looking for a fire stone, a shelter, and food – all at once. Always, always you look for food. There, up along the edge of the clearing – you see those stumps?'

Derek nodded.

'Those will be a good bet for grubworms later.'

'Grubworms?'

'Sure. Bears eat them – love to eat them. I can't eat

37

them yet, but by about the third day if we don't find something else or get some fish they'll probably be looking pretty good.'

'Grubworms?'

Brian smiled. 'I thought you did this survival thing once before.'

'Oh, we ate lizards and snakes and stuff like that – they always have the course in the desert. Or did until now. I think it will change. And you always read about people eating ants and grasshoppers, but I never ate a grubworm.'

'You don't chew them,' Brian said. 'I think that would be too much. Just to chew one up, guts and all. They're too soft and, well, just too soft. But if you wrap them in leaves and swallow them whole . . . '

'Right,' Derek nodded and wrote in the notebook. 'Grubworms.'

Brian stopped and turned to Derek. 'Food is everything.'

'What do you mean?'

'Just that. Out here, in nature, in the world, food is everything. All the other parts of what we are, what everything is, don't matter without food. I read somewhere that all of what man is, everything man has always been or will be, all the thoughts and dreams and sex and hate and every little and big thing is dependent on six inches of topsoil and rain when you need it to make a crop grow – food.'

'You sound like you've thought this out.'

'That's *all* I did – think of food. You watch other animals, birds, fish, even down to ants – they spend all their time working at food. Getting something to eat. That's what nature is, really – getting food. And when you're

38

out here, having to live, you look for food. Food first. Food. *Food*.'

They moved through the day that way. During mid-morning they found some raspberries growing in a brush-pile. It was not a thick stand – it would maybe have been enough for one person, but with two it was skimpy – still, there were some and they worked through the brush in their underwear, eating every berry they could find.

They also found some chokecherries – what Brian had called gut cherries – but Brian shook his head. 'Later, if we have to, and then in small amounts.'

Brian kept moving along the lake, waiting, walking, and waiting, and he realised at length what he was waiting for – what was in the back of his mind.

Luck.

You move and you watch and you work hard and you just keep doing that until luck comes. If it's bad luck you ride it out and if it comes the other way and you have good luck you're ready for it.

They had good luck in the middle of the afternoon. And as so often seems to happen, the good luck came about because of bad luck.

EIGHT

Brian had moved out ahead, down and to the right of Derek, and was working closer to the edge of the lake. Derek worked up and away from the lake, looking for more berries as they moved.

'Stay in sight of me,' Brian had told him. 'Don't get away from the lake so far that you can't see, and if you run into a bear don't look into his eyes.'

'Bear?'

'They hunt for food, too, and eat berries. We'll probably see one. Just back away and don't look at them – I read that it's a threat when you do that.'

'Bear?'

Brian was glad to see that his warning had been taken and Derek was always within sight.

Here the land rose as they approached the northern end of the lake. It came up in a low roll that made a sizable hill next to the lake. Because of this rise and the freezing and thawing of the lake, the movement of the ice each winter, the land had been cut away, washed still further away by heavy rains – Brian could see the work of last night's rain – and all this chewing at the side of the hill had left something close to a small cliff.

It wasn't terribly high – thirty feet or so – but it was steep and very unstable, the edge loose and soft from the rain.

Brian had moved close to the edge. Down below he

could see into the green water of the lake and there were fish moving and the sight made him realise how hungry he was becoming. It had been over a day now – they had eaten normally the day before when they flew to the lake – and the hunger was becoming demanding.

He turned to see Derek, who was coming up the back of the hill. 'See the fish — '

Brian had come too close to the soft soil at the edge, and before he could finish the sentence, the bank let go.

He dropped like an anvil, his finger still pointing at the fish. Halfway down the face of the cut there was a small outcropping of soil and rocks mixed, held in place because it was made of clay and chalk bound together, and Brian hit this mound on his stomach. Hard.

'Ooomph!' He heard himself sound like the air going out of a tire, then he bounced up and sideways and continued on down to the bottom in a shower of mud and rocks, to where a small gravel beach led into the lake.

I don't think I'll move, he thought, lying flat on his face. *Ever again.*

Derek was by his side in moments, frowning in worry. 'Are you hurt?'

I wonder why people ask that, Brian thought. *Did he think I could do this and not hurt?*

But he shook his head. 'No. At least I don't think so . . .'

He rose, or put his hands down to push himself up, and as he made the move he noticed the rocks around him on the beach. Most of them were round and smooth, rubbled by wind and water and weather and time, but mixed in with them were black, hardened shards.

Where he'd fallen there were fresh ones, not weath-

41

ered, and he saw that they had come from the bank where he had bounced.

'Look,' Brian held up one of the black stones. It was chipped and layered. 'I think it might be the same kind of stone I used to make fire with the hatchet.'

'Flint,' Derek said. 'I think it is.'

Brian took out his knife, opened it and locked the blade, and struck the back of the hard steel against the sharp edge of the flint. Three, four times he hit and finally there were sparks.

He looked up, smiling. 'No more mosquitoes.'

He took two of the larger black stones and they went to find a campsite, and here, too, there was the waiting for luck.

They walked nearly halfway around the lake, looking always as well for food. As they worked past the northern end of the lake they came on low brush filled with small nuts. These he knew were hazelnuts, and they stopped to pick and eat some. They were ripe, or very close, just shy of being dry, and the worms and squirrels had been at them, but they still found enough to cut the edge off their hunger. They used rocks to smash them and spent over an hour bashing rocks and nibbling at the small chunks of nutmeat, which tasted almost sweet.

It was then approaching evening and Brian knew they would need a shelter of some kind and a fire, before dark and the evening horde of insects found them.

Then, coming out of a stand of thick willows, they found it.

In some ancient time, an enormous tree had fallen in a giant wind. The tree had been growing on the side of a small hill, which was made on a rocky shelf. As the tree went over it pulled earth, balled in its roots, with it, and made a large hole back in, under the shelf of rocks.

Time had done the rest. The tree was long rotted and gone to worms, the soil had filtered somewhat back into the hole and taken grass seeds, and what was left was a large depression in the side of the hill with an overhanging shelf of rock. On each side of the depression there were large trees – white pines that went towering up and shaded the whole place to make it feel like a quiet garden.

It was not perfect, not as nice as Brian had had on the L-shaped lake. But it was good enough, far better than nothing, and to cap it off, there was a small spring of water to the side of the overhang, where a fissure of rock let water work out in a trickle that made its way down to the lake.

'Home,' Brian said.

Derek looked at the depression. 'It looks like a hole – what do we do to make it livable?'

'Beds and a fire. You use pine boughs to make the beds.' He showed Derek how to cut the boughs and stick them point down to make a soft bed. 'You do that and I'll work on a fire.'

'I need to watch you do that,' Derek said. 'So I can write about it.'

Brian nodded and set out to find what he needed.

He would never forget the first fire, what it had meant to him – as important as it must have been to early man – and he approached making a fire now almost as a religious experience.

You could not hurry it, he knew. Fire would come only when it wanted to come, and only when there was a good bed for it, a home for it.

He found some birches near the shoreline and shredded

43

dry birch bark with his fingernails until it was like hair. He kept adding to this until he had a ball of fluff three inches in diameter.

To this he added some pulverised, dried grass, worked almost into flour, and when it was all together, he gently used his finger to make a hole in the middle.

A home for the fire, he thought. A place for it to live.

Derek had watched all of this with intense interest, writing in his notebook from time to time, underlining things, nodding.

Brian set aside the tinder and found some dry pine twigs, as small as matches. When he had a good pile of these, broken and lined up for use, he searched for slightly larger dry wood and still larger until he had a pile as high as his knees.

In all of this he was silent, thinking only of the fire, but he turned to Derek now. 'You can't have too much wood. Ever. And you should always have dried wood stashed back in some safe place, along with tinder . . . ' He paused, thinking, remembering.

'What is it?' Derek asked.

'Fire. It's so . . . so alive. Such an important thing to us. Back there in the world we don't know that. But when I got home last time I tried to read about what it was like, you know, before we got everything we have now. In colonial times they kept people awake just to watch the fires, and in ancient times the most important person in the tribe was called the fire watcher.'

Derek wrote it down and Brian smiled. Something about Derek walking around all day looking for berries and nuts, carrying a briefcase like a business executive, seemed ridiculous. But he meant what he was doing and Brian liked him more and more all the time. When he'd fallen and Derek had kneeled next to him, he had been genuinely worried.

Fire.

There was a lowering of light now and evening would not be long, accompanied by the waiting bugs.

He and Derek made a small fire pit in front of the overhang. Then Brian put the tinder on the ground in the pit so that the flame cup was aimed upward.

Over this he held the piece of flint.

He struck it with the knife and nothing came.

Naturally, he thought. If it were easy, everybody would want to do this.

He hit again and again and finally the sparks came. Now he slammed the stone with the back of the knife blade with renewed force, again and again until a small shower of sparks fell into the cup.

Quickly he raised the tinder in his hand, blowing gently, softly on the sparks, watching as they became glowing holes in the tinder and the holes grew, became red, turned to coals and finally, blowing as he put it back on the ground, smoke curling up into his eyes, there came the tiny flicker of new flame.

Hello, he thought – *hello, flame*. Fire.

He fed small twigs to the flame, crossing them and recrossing them until the fire was full, healthy. Then he added larger sticks and still larger until they filled the pit and there was the crackling sound of a full fire.

Brian settled back on his haunches and smiled; looked up at Derek, who was also smiling.

Brian gestured around with his hand. 'No more mosquitoes – the smoke keeps them away. It doesn't even take much, just a little blowing around. But we need more wood.'

45

They took the next hour to gather wood, stacking it until they had a large pile to the side of the camp, and Derek used the time to cut pine boughs for beds as well. When it was late, and they finally lay back to rest, they had done much to make the overhang a home.

Brian went to sleep on his side. The last thing he heard before he dozed was the sound of a wolf. He heard Derek rise.

'It's a wolf,' Brian said. 'Far away, just singing. Besides, wolves don't bother you. You can go back to sleep.'

And Derek did, rolling over, his breathing even, and Brian let sleep come again.

NINE

Brian stood away from the fish trap and shook his head.

Nothing was the same, really.

It was a beautiful day, with the mid-afternoon sun shining down on them, and he thought of what the problem could be, what was wrong.

It had somehow turned into one big happy camping trip.

We might as well have a cooler full of soft drinks and sandwiches, Brian thought.

They'd been at the lake three days, but it looked like they'd been there a year. The camp was squared away and neat. Derek had called in on the radio and told the world they were all right, telling them to pass the information on to Brian's parents – Brian thought his mother might worry if she knew about them sending the gear back. Then they had enhanced the beds and made them deep and soft with more boughs, there was enough firewood for a month, and they had made birch-bark containers to hold extra hazelnuts and berries.

They'd found blueberries and raspberries and plums. On this side of the lake the forest was more open and the plums and nuts and berries seemed to thrive in the light and heat.

Wild plums. They were a little green, but even so, Brian couldn't believe how sweet and rich they were –

like small, domestic plums, with a little more tang to them.

Brian had made a bow, used a strip from his belt for a string, and had shown Derek how to shoot fish, then how to use the guts from one fish to bait the others into a trap made of stones; and they soon had more fish than they needed. Brian found a clam bed and they had actually eaten one meal – clams steamed around the fire, nuts, and berries – that left them full.

Full.

Plus, they had more clams stored and plenty of fish left in the trap and knew the locations of several ruffed grouse. There were rabbits and squirrels all over the place, and if they had to they could make it a year or two, and it felt wrong.

All wrong.

He shook his head again and moved back by the fire pit. Derek was sitting on his bed by the fire, feeding an occasional stick to the fire to keep it going, writing in his notebook. He looked up as Brian walked into the shelter, and saw him shaking his head.

'What's the matter?'

Brian shrugged. 'I don't know – it's just wrong, I think.'

'What do you mean – wrong?'

Brian looked around at the shelter, the comfort, the food, the fire, the lake. 'All this. We're so . . . so ready. So calm. It doesn't work, somehow. None of it works.'

'I still don't know for sure what you're talking about. We've done it. In four days you've shown me how to live in the wilderness with nothing but a knife. I've got tons of notes to take back and teach from – I think you're wrong.'

'But this isn't how it works,' Brian said. 'It isn't this smooth and easy. You don't just fly in and get set on a perfect lake and have all the food you want and have it all come this easy. It isn't real.'

Derek leaned back, put his hands in back of his head, and looked at Brian.

'There's not a thing to make it rough . . . nothing wrong. In a real situation, like when I was here before, there were things wrong – going wrong. The plane didn't land and set me on the shore. It crashed. A man was dead. I was hurt. I didn't know anything. Nothing at all. I was, maybe, close to death and now we're out here going la-de-da, I've got a fish; la-de-da, there are some more berries.'

'Tension.' Derek said. 'It lacks tension.'

Brian nodded. 'Maybe – but that's not all. I don't think you can *teach* what you want to teach.'

'But they do – they teach survival.'

'No. I think they tell people what to do and maybe you can tell them some of what we do. But that doesn't teach them *how* to live, *how* to do it, does it? You'd have to bring each person here and drop them in the lake and let them swim out and drag up the shore and try to live, to really *teach* them how to do it. Every single one.'

'But that's impossible.'

Brian nodded. 'I know. But I don't think it will work unless you do it that way. You can tell, but you can't really teach.'

'Tension,' Derek said again, leaning forward and writing in his notebook again. 'You need the tension created by the emergency.'

49

And they settled in for the rest of the day and that night, and later Brian would remember what they had said – how it needed tension – and wish he had not thought it at all.

TEN

Brian awakened suddenly, and listened, and smelled.

For a moment he could not tell what had brought him up from sleep. They had banked the fire well and the coals would last until morning. It was still warm and red, giving off a little smoke. There were no bugs, the night cool wasn't too cold, no animals prowled, and he could find nothing wrong and was closing his eyes to sleep again when he heard it.

The far-off sound of thunder. Not loud; low and rumbling. He could smell rain coming, but that should pose no problem. The storms and the wind came from the north-north-west and they had the hill in back to protect them. With the overhang facing south and being on the side of the hill, the rain wouldn't bother them. In fact, they'd had an evening of soft rain and nothing had come in the shelter – not a drop. And with the storm blowing any rain away from the opening, they should stay dry and safe.

Brian put a couple of pieces of wood on the fire to make sure it kept going, added a handful of green leaves to make smoke and keep the mosquitoes down, checked to see that Derek was still sleeping, and lay back on his bed.

Maybe the storm wouldn't even hit them. He remembered the tornado that had caught him before and decided he wouldn't worry. The odds against getting hit twice by

51

anything as wild as a tornado were huge, and there was nothing they could do anyway, except just hope that it would miss them. He remembered the sound the tornado had made – the wild roaring – and the storm it had come from, and this was different.

A summer rainstorm with soft thunder – it didn't seem anything to worry about and certainly nothing to keep him awake. He went back to sleep, slipping into a light doze.

Things moved in and out – he dreamed that he was talking to Derek, saying in the dream that he thought they should use the radio to call the plane and cancel the rest of the 'operation,' as Derek kept calling it in the dream, because it didn't seem to prove anything.

He was awakened by an explosion.

It seemed to come from inside his skull, inside his thinking, inside the dream: a sharp crack, so loud that he snapped awake, rolled over, and was on his feet, moving to the back of the shelter without thinking, without knowing he was moving.

It was thunder.

But not like he'd heard before, not like he'd ever heard. It was around them, exploding around them, the lightning cracking around the shelter, so close it seemed to Brian that it came from inside him.

'What — '

He knew that he opened his mouth, that he made sound, but he could hear nothing except the *whack-crack* of the thunder, see nothing but images frozen in the split-instants of brilliance from the lightning.

Like a camera taking pictures by a strobe light, things would seem frozen in time, caught and frozen, and then

52

there would be another flash and things would be different.

Derek was moving.

In one flash he was still on his bed, but raised, his jacket falling away from where he'd had it as a blanket, as he rose.

Darkness.

Then the next flash of light and he was on his knees.

Darkness.

Then he was leaning forward and his hand was out, reaching for his briefcase and radio next to the bed, one finger out, his face concentrating; and Brian thought, no, don't reach, stay low; and he might have yelled it, screamed it, but it didn't matter. No sound could be loud enough to get over the thunder.

There was a slashing, new, impossibly loud crack as lightning seemed to hit the shelter itself and Brian saw the top of the pine next to the opening suddenly explode and felt/saw the bolt come roaring down the tree, burning and splitting and splintering the wood and bark, and he saw it hit Derek.

Camera image.

Some *thing*, some blueness of heat and light and raw power seemed to jump from the tree to the briefcase and radio and enter Derek's hand. All in the same part of a second it hit him and his back arched, snapped him erect, and then it seemed to fill the whole shelter and slammed into Brian as well.

He saw the blueness, almost a ball of energy, the crack/flash of colour that came from inside his mind, inside his life, and then he was back and down and saw nothing more.

53

ELEVEN

Before his eyes opened there was light through the eye-lids, bright light, but they didn't want to open and focus. He tasted things, smelled things. Something was burned, there was the stink of something burned. Hair. Burned hair.

It smelled awful.

He opened his eyes wide, blinked, forced them to work and saw that he was on his back, looking at the stone-layered ceiling of the overhang.

It was daylight, broad daylight, and he wondered why it was that he would be lying on his back on the dirt, looking at the ceiling in the middle of the day.

Then he remembered.

Parts of it: the sound, the light, the thunder, and the slamming and cracking of it; and he was afraid. He did not know what he was afraid of at first, he was just afraid, and then, finally, he remembered Derek.

It had hit him.

He had seen it hit Derek.

He rolled on his side. His body felt stiff, mashed into the ground, and the sudden movement made his vision blur.

There.

He saw Derek – or the form of Derek. He was face-down on his bed, his right hand out, his left arm back and down his side. Blurred, he was all blurred and asleep

– how could he be all blurred? Brian shook his head, tried to focus.

Derek was still asleep. How strange, Brian thought – how strange that Derek should still be asleep in the bright daylight, and he knew then that Derek was not sleeping, but did not want to think of the other thing.

Let's reason it out, he thought, his mind as blurred as his vision. Reason it all out. Derek was reaching for the radio and briefcase and the lightning hit the tree next to the shelter and came down the tree and across the air and into Derek and he fell . . .

No.

He was still asleep.

He wasn't that other thing. Not that other word.

But Brian's eyes began to clear then and saw that Derek was lying with his head to the side and that it was facing Brian and the eyes weren't closed.

They were open.

He was on his side not moving and his eyes were open and Brian thought how strange it was that he would sleep that way – mashed on his stomach.

He knew Derek wasn't sleeping.

He knew.

'No . . . '

He couldn't be. Couldn't be . . . dead. Not Derek.

Finally, he accepted it.

Brian rose to his hands and knees, stiff and with great slowness, and crawled across the floor of the shelter to where Derek lay.

The large man lay on his stomach as he'd dropped, his head turned to the left. The eyes were not fully open, but partially lidded, and the pupils stared blankly, unfocused toward the back of the shelter.

Brian touched his cheek. He remembered how when the pilot had his heart attack he had felt cool – the dead skin had felt cool.

Derek's skin did not have the coolness, it felt warm; and Brian kneeled next to him and saw that he was breathing.

Tiny little breaths, his chest barely rising and falling, but he was breathing, the air going in and out, and he was not the other word – not dead – and Brian leaned over him.

'Derek?'

There was no answer, no indication that Derek had heard him.

'Derek. Can you hear anything I'm saying?'

Still no sign, no movement.

So, Brian thought – so he's what? He's knocked out. He got hit and he's knocked out and if I wait and make him comfortable he'll come out of it.

That was it. Just knocked out.

Derek's head looked twisted at an uncomfortable angle and Brian moved Derek's body on to its side and set his head – the neck felt rubbery and loose – on his rolled-up jacket for a pillow. As he did he saw the briefcase and radio.

The radio.

There it was, right there on the briefcase; and if there was ever a need for it, it was now.

He picked it up, turned the switch on.

'Katie One, this is Katie Two, over.'

His mother's name. It was a small thing, a way to include his mother. They used her name as the call sign and Derek had shown Brian how to use the radio, the correct procedure in case of an emergency.

Like now.

'Katie One, this is Katie Two, over.'

Nothing. He turned the squelch control down and listened for the hiss of static, but there was nothing. Not even noise.

Again.

'Katie One, this is Katie Two, over.'

Dead air. He saw, then, that next to where the antennae came out of the case, there was a small discoloured spot on the plastic. It was a burn mark. The radio was made to be used outdoors, tough, with a weatherproof case around it, and when he opened the outside case he saw that the lightning had hit the radio as well as Derek and him.

There was a jagged line burned in the plastic on the back and even without opening the case and seeing the inside he knew the radio was blown.

What to do? Think. He couldn't think right.

He put the radio down and turned back to Derek. There was no change at all – no movement except for the short rise and fall of his chest with his breathing. The eyes were still partially opened, as they had been.

Think.

What did he know that could help?

Lightning had hit the tree next to the overhang, come down the side – he saw where the pine bark was burned and literally blown from the tree – and then must have come out on a root or jumped away from the tree somehow.

No, that wasn't right. He'd read somewhere that lightning struck *up*, not down – moved from the ground up.

Somehow it had come from the ground, through Derek and the radio and him to the tree, and then up, except that it seemed to come down and Derek shouldn't have reached out, shouldn't have risen . . .

He shook his head. Stupid. None of that mattered.

Electrical shock. What did you do when there was electrical shock?

C.P.R.

To get them breathing again, you had to give them C.P.R. – except that Derek was breathing already.

Heart. He should check the heart.

He put his fingers on Derek's wrist, but couldn't find the pulse – but when he checked his own he couldn't find that either. He put his ear to Derek's chest and heard the heart thumping. He tried to time it, but couldn't transpose the number of beats per minute measured on his digital watch into a pulse rate because he couldn't think.

Think.

The lightning came, took the tree, then Derek, the radio, him – and they were all knocked down and out.

There it was – maybe Derek was just knocked out and would come to in a little while.

Somehow he knew that wasn't true. Something in the way Derek looked made the condition look like more than just being knocked out. Yet Brian wanted it to be, wanted it to be so much that he forced himself to believe it.

Derek was breathing evenly – short breaths, but even – and his heart was beating regularly.

He was just knocked out.

Brian would make him comfortable and then wait next to him. Wait for him to come to.

He would wait.

TWELVE

The rest of that day and through the night, he kneeled next to Derek.

Waiting.

He only moved to get a drink and eat some berries and go to the bathroom, the rest of the time he kneeled next to Derek, putting a piece of wood on the fire now and then to keep it going, waiting. Waiting.

And he knew.

He knew that Derek was not just unconscious, was more seriously hurt than that, and still he did not know what to do.

Or if he could do anything.

The radio was gone. They had made a schedule that said they would check in once a week or so – it was very loose – and that they would call if there was an emergency. Derek had just done the weekly check-in the afternoon before, so they wouldn't think it odd that there were no calls. The bush-plane headquarters said they would keep their radio on around the clock, but not necessarily manned all the time, so even if he had a radio, Brian might not be able to get them right away. Of course, he could call any other airplane and report the emergency.

If he had a radio.

So he could not call for help, and they would not worry for another week or so, when Derek did not call in. There they were, where they sat.

Derek was down, unconscious.

In a coma.

There. *That* word came. He had been afraid of the word *death* before and now this word, *coma*. He'd have to stop that, have to face things better than he was facing them. He knew almost nothing of medical terms or what happened to people with severe shock, and knew less than nothing about comas.

He'd seen movies about people in comas for months and months or years and years and then they would suddenly snap out of it and wonder how long they'd been asleep.

In the night, next to Derek, he tried to will him awake. *Snap awake now and ask how long you've been sleeping. Now. And we'll laugh and talk about how close the lightning came.*

But it did not work.

Derek did not awaken, made no change of any kind. Somewhere just before dawn, when the first light of false dawn was making the western side of the lake come into view, Brian finally accepted it.

Derek was in a coma and was apparently not going to snap out of it. At least not soon.

That left everything, everything on Brian, and for a moment he felt a touch of anger and resentment.

The woods.

The damn woods.

Last time he'd almost died, would have died, except for luck, and now this – this again. All this dumped on him just because he tried to do the right thing, and he didn't even want to do it. Anyway, Derek was so dumb that he raised up and reached out when he should have stayed low and . . . and . . . and . . .

Listen to me, he thought. *If I were talking out loud, I'd be whining.*

Derek gets hit and I act like I'm the one getting messed up.

It was this way, he thought. Derek was unconscious and it seemed to be a coma – or something like a coma.

He did not seem to be coming out of it.

The radio did not work and Brian could not call for help.

So, then what?

They might come looking in a week or ten days. Could he stay here with Derek for a week or ten days and wait for them?

Could he *not* stay? What choices did he have?

If he stayed and Derek didn't regain consciousness, how long would he . . . last? If he didn't get food and water, could he stay alive?

They never talked about that in movies or on television. They never said what they did with people in a coma. Fed them through tubes, probably.

But he couldn't do that.

He had to try to put food and water down Derek's throat, and if he did that he might choke him and kill him.

So he couldn't really do that, either.

'So, then,' he said aloud, speaking to and not to Derek at the same time. 'What can I do?'

He had kneeled next to Derek almost all night, and when he tried to stand, his knees almost buckled. He rolled sideways and flexed his legs, and while he was rolled to the side he smelled it.

Oh, yes – I'd forgotten that kind of thing – the bathroom. Derek would, of course, have to go to the bathroom – his body functions would keep going. Or would they? Yes, apparently they would.

There was that too. To take care of Derek, truly take care of him – he'd never had to do anything like it before, take care of someone.

Himself, sure, but he'd never been really responsible for some other person, and he wondered what to do – what a person did.

The anger had passed, but he felt immense frustration at his helplessness.

It had to be done. He had to clean Derek, take care of him, take care of another human being. Look at it that way, he thought – not Derek, but another person. He had to clean this helpless person – if he kept it detached, maybe he could do it.

Why would it be so hard anyway?

He unfastened Derek's pants and the smell grew stronger.

'Oh, God.'

He fought the nausea down, controlled it, turned Derek over and held his breath and used grass to clean him. Then he pulled the pants up and put him on his side again.

Parents – how did parents do it? It was horrible – how could they do it? He used sticks to carry it and the grass to the hole they had dug for a bathroom and covered it with dirt, then went down to the lake and washed his hands again and again until he could hold them to his face and not smell anything. When they were clean and he could breathe normally without choking, he went back to Derek.

Comfort – he could do what he could to make Derek

more comfortable. Brian moved him and rearranged the pine boughs to make a softer bed.

Then he pulled Derek on to his back on the new boughs, but was alarmed when Derek seemed to begin to choke or breathe strangely, and he put him back on his side.

So, nothing.

Nothing he could do, not really.

It was full light now, warm, with the sun drying the rain off the grass. A warm summer morning with birds singing, Brian thought, looking across the mirrored surface of the lake – a beautiful summer morning with birds singing and fish jumping on the lake and everything perfect, except for this one thing. This one little thing.

Derek was in a coma.

THIRTEEN

Somewhere, Brian thought, somewhere he'd heard something about comas. He must have. Something more than he could remember. But it had to be in his mind, in his thinking, and if it was there he must be able to get it out.

He spent the morning trying to remember what he knew, but nothing came.

It was like being asleep, except that you didn't wake up, he thought. Everything kept working, but you couldn't eat or drink.

He had been moving from the lake to the shelter with a birch-bark cone full of water when it hit him.

They could wait all week, wait nine or ten days for the plane to come – or he could. He knew that people had gone that long without food. Derek would lose some weight, but he wouldn't starve to death in that time.

But Brian was sure Derek could not go that long without water. Two, three days, maybe four, then he would be in trouble. Somewhere he'd heard or read or seen that the human body couldn't go that long without water.

And it had already been one day, going on two days.

He could try getting Derek to drink. If he could get water in him he would last. His breathing had steadied still more and his heart rate was close to normal. Brian had finally settled enough to measure it and calculate that it was running about sixty-five beats per minute. He remembered something about the rate supposing to be

64

seventy-two, so Derek was low, but it was still working all right.

Brian made a small spoonlike holder out of birch bark. With this he dipped water from the cone, which he had propped next to Derek's head, and he put a small bit of water into the unconscious man's mouth.

The effect was immediate and explosive.

'*Charrsst!*'

Derek choked instantly, and reflex action took over and he coughed, spraying water and spit in Brian's face. The choking continued and Brian frantically pulled Derek's head over to the side, held his face down and pounded on his back – all he knew to do.

It seemed to last forever and Brian was terrified that he had killed Derek. One mistake, one thing wrong, and he was choking to death.

But finally the water cleared from Derek's throat and the coughing stopped, though his breathing was still ragged.

'So, you can't drink.' Brian settled Derek's head back on to the rolled-up jacket. 'That doesn't make all this any easier.'

At first he felt strange, talking to Derek when there was no indication that he could be heard. Then he remembered his mother reading a story in a paper and telling him about a girl that had been in a coma for months – please, he thought, dear God, don't let Derek be under that long – and when she recovered she said that while she was in the coma she could hear people talking. She could hear and understand, but could not answer, and he thought Derek might be the same.

'Derek?' He leaned close to Derek's face. 'Can you hear me?'

There was no sign.

'Can you move your eyelids? If you hear me, move your eyelids.'

Nothing. The eyes were half open, filled with tears that came constantly. Apparently the body was trying to keep them from drying out, because Derek could not blink.

He sat up, then stood and looked at the sky. *I can't do this*, he thought. *I can't do this alone. I just can't . . .*

He looked down at Derek again, shook his head. 'I don't know what to do.'

And he realised then that he was wrong – it wasn't like last time. He wasn't alone.

There was Derek. Maybe if he talked to him, spoke aloud to him – maybe it might help.

'Here it is,' Brian said, squatting again, moving a stick in the dirt. 'There's no way anybody will come for at least a week, and maybe longer. Maybe ten days. I don't think you can . . . I don't think it would be good to go that long without water. I can't get you to drink because I think you'll choke. So.'

'So.' He repeated, shrugging, drawing a big zero in the dirt. 'I don't know what to do.'

He threw the stick down in exasperation. It hit the ground harder than he meant, then bounced and skipped into Derek's briefcase.

Brian saw it as if for the first time. He'd forgotten about it in the crisis and went to it. 'What have you got in here?'

It was not locked and he opened it with the two sliding thumb releases on either end of the handle edge.

Inside, there were spiral notebooks. They weren't anything special – the kind with ruled lines and the twisted wire holding the edge – and each of them was numbered.

He opened number one.

66

'Arrived,' he read aloud. 'Brian demanded that we leave all the gear in the plane or it would ruin the whole experiment.'

Oh, yes, Brian thought – I did that. Oh, God, I did that, didn't I? I stuck my little foot down and dug in and got stubborn and set all this up. What was there? Food and shelter and a gun and all the things I didn't think we'd need that would make this easier.

'I admire his ethics.' He finished reading the first day. He put the notebook down. 'You do, eh? Admire me – the guy who made us lose all that gear?'

He felt like he was prying and decided not to read any more of the notebooks. He started to close the briefcase and saw that there was a folding accordion-style section that collapsed back into the lid.

There was something in the section and he pulled out a folded paper. When he opened it he saw that it was the map.

The same map they had looked at with Brian's mother. He saw the lake, saw where they had circled it with her, showing where they would be, how . . . how *located* it looked. How easy to see and find and locate.

Derek had had two copies of the map and he'd left one with Brian's mother. 'So you can always tell right where we are.'

Brian remembered sitting there, his mother smiling. All her questions answered, all her doubts gone.

And now look at them.

Derek had brought the other map and kept it when Brian dug his heels in and told him to send everything but the radio back and in some relief Brian had spread the map gratefully on the back of the briefcase – thinking it would help – but now he shook his head and started to fold it. What difference did it make if he knew where they were? It wouldn't help them.

Then he looked at the lake again, saw how it lay in the wide, flat greenness – how there were many lakes around it.

And he saw the river.

FOURTEEN

He had noticed it before, of course – when they went over the map in his house and when they had first landed. But in the largeness of the country shown on the map, the massive forest the map showed, the river was a small thing, and he had negated it.

It wound out the bottom of the lake, the southern end, and headed southeast down into the lakes below and was lost, and he had not followed it except to note the name.

The Necktie River.

'Isn't that a funny name,' his mother had said, and Derek had laughed.

'There are lakes named Eunice, or Bootsock – there are so many lakes and rivers, the original mapmakers just made up names as they went. The person drawing the map was probably wearing a tie and thought it would make a good name. Many of them aren't named at all – just numbered.'

The Necktie River, Brian saw, led south and down and drew his eyes away from the lake.

The map was laid out in square five-thousand-meter grids – five-kilometer squares – and he saw that in some places the river wound back almost on itself inside the same five thousand square meters. But in other places it ran straight for a considerable distance and he followed it, through smaller lakes and what he thought must be swamps, through the darker green portions that meant heavier forest.

It kept going south to the edge of the map, where it was folded, and he unfolded the next section and spread it in the sun. He did not know why the river drew him, pulled at him.

Then, halfway through the second page, he saw it. The river had grown all along, got wider so that it made a respectable blue cut across the map and where it made a large bend, cutting back nearly straight east, there was a small circle drawn and the words:

Brannock Trading Post.

Leading away from Brannock's Post there was a double line heading down and to the southwest. When he found the symbol for the double line on the map's legend he saw that it stood for an improved gravel road.

There would be people there.

Right there, on the map, at Brannock's Trading Post there would be people. They wouldn't have a road or name the place or make it a dot on the map unless there were people there. A trading post would have people.

Which, Brian thought, doesn't mean a thing.

He wasn't at Brannock's Trading Post. He was here.

Yet he couldn't take his eyes off the spot on the map. It was there, on the same map – just there. And he refolded the map so it would show the lake where they were and the trading post at the same time. He used his fingers to make a divider and measured it straight down, but it didn't mean anything.

Then he remembered that the grids stood for five kilometers each, and when he counted the numbers of grids between the lake and Brannock's he came up with about sixteen squares.

'So how far is that?' he said to Derek. 'Five times sixteen – maybe eighty, eighty-five kilometers.'

But that was straight – in a straight line southeast.

The river was nowhere near straight, looping back and forth and actually flowing slightly north back along itself at one point.

He started counting, measuring the river as it turned through each five-kilometer square, marking each ten kilometers in the dirt with a line through it, then the next set of ten. It was involved and took him some time, but finally he was done.

He counted them.

'One hundred and fifty kilometers,' he said. 'One point six kilometers to a mile. Just under a hundred miles.'

He looked at Derek, who did not move, who made no sign.

'There are people just under a hundred miles from here.'

But what good did that do?

'Here it is – I could leave you and try to follow the river out and bring help back.'

Which, he thought, sounded insane. There were animals. They would come, and if they thought Derek was dead . . . He was defenseless. They might attack him. Even eat him. Even small things – ants, bugs.

'I can't leave you.'

Brian looked at the map again. It was there, the answer was there. Brannock's Trading Post was the answer and the river was the answer, but he didn't see how.

He couldn't leave Derek.

He couldn't leave Derek . . .

What if he took Derek with him?

He said it aloud. 'What if we went out together?'

On the face of it, it sounded like madness. Haul a man in a coma nearly a hundred miles out of the wilderness on a river.

You could say that, Brian thought, but there was a lot of difference between saying it and doing it.

How could he?

The river. If he had a boat . . . or a raft.

If he made a raft and put Derek on the raft, there might be a way he could make the run and take Derek out, get him to the trading post and to help.

And even as he said it he knew it was crazy. A hundred miles on a wilderness river with a raft, hauling a grown man who would be nothing but dead weight, was impossible.

He would have dropped it, except that he looked up from the map and saw the truth then; looked up and saw Derek with his eyes half open and not seeing, awake but not truly living, the minutes of his life moving past and Brian knew that he really didn't have any choice.

If he stayed Derek would die of thirst in two, perhaps three days. Well before the week or ten days that would pass before the pilot came looking to see what happened.

If he stayed, Derek would die.

If he made the run, took Derek down the river, at least there was a chance.

He had no choice.

FIFTEEN

Time was everything now – once the decision was made, time was vital. But Brian took a minute to scan the map once more and do some mental calculating, and it didn't come up too terrible.

Say it was a hundred miles by river.

When they'd landed they'd come down next to where the river left the lake, and Brian had watched the current as it flowed away. It seemed to move about as fast as a person walked – maybe three miles an hour. Of course, that didn't mean that it would continue to flow at that speed, but it would probably be about the same.

If he could get into the current and move with it and stay with it, a hundred miles would take thirty-five or forty hours.

He studied it closer on the map and noted that it grew wider as it flowed and that in some places it moved through hilly country – there were contour lines on the map close together, which meant steeper hills. Here the current might even be a little faster.

A day and a half, he thought. Then he said it aloud for Derek. 'A day and a half. A long day and a half, but if we keep moving, stay in the river and don't stop, we should make the trading post in a day and a half. Maybe two days.' And that, he thought without saying, is a lot better than seven or eight.

A lot better than dying.

There were two places where the river ran into lakes and out the other end, and many smaller ponds and what might be swamps where the river moved through a centre of a small body of water. They would slow him down.

He could not judge how much, but none of them were large, and if he stayed on the edge and used a pole he should be able to keep moving well enough not to lose too much time.

Time.

He was sitting, reading, looking at the map, and there wasn't time for it.

He needed to build a raft.

He checked Derek one more time, made certain his breathing was regular and that his heart was beating steadily and then moved off down the side of the lake, looking for wood.

The problem was not wood so much as the lack of a tool. When he'd made the raft before to go out to the plane he'd had his hatchet, and he missed it terribly now. After he'd been rescued and gone home, his mother had put the hatchet in a glass case in the living room, where she kept the china handed down by her grandmother. He'd looked at it as he'd left the house, but they had decided that having a hatchet might not be realistic.

'Lots of people carry a knife of some kind,' Derek had said. 'But how many have a hatchet on their belt?'

So all he had was a knife – well, two knives, actually. He had Derek's knife as well. He'd almost forgotten that.

But even two knives wouldn't help him cut through logs.

There was wood all over the place. Wind storms over the years had knocked down pines and spruce trees and many of them were the right diameter to use for making a raft – six or eight inches and straight. But they were for the most part too long, or still connected to the root structure, which made them impossible to use.

But Brian moved along the lake, up from the shore and back, and finally he found a stand of large poplars where beavers had been working.

He knew almost nothing of beavers except that they lived in the water, chewed trees down, and looked cute when he saw them swimming in the water. Except for pictures he'd never seen one on dry land, but he'd seen how they took trees down and this stand of poplars was a good example. In a hundred-yard circle there wasn't a tree standing.

There were pointed stumps everywhere, with tooth marks on them, and dropped trees fallen across each other so thickly that it looked like giants had started to play pick-up-sticks and walked away before finishing the game.

The beavers had been working at the grove for some time – probably years – and they had not only dropped the trees, many of them the right diameter, but they had cut the limbs off and dragged them down pathways to the lake and cut some of the tree trunks in sections between eight and ten or twelve feet long, apparently to make them easier to move.

It's like I hired them, Brian thought, looking at all the fallen poplars – just to cut them down for me.

The older trees, which had been cut down the year or two before, were well dried out, and when Brian rolled and skidded them down to the lake he found that they floated well. Four of them side by side held him up easily when he used his arms to hold them together and crawled on top of them. He got wet, but they held him.

Of course, Derek was a lot heavier and the two of them together heavier still, but eight or ten of them should do it. And there were many the right size and length. He had only to select the ones he wanted.

He worked hard for a solid half hour, then ran to check on Derek. He was still the same, and Brian jogged back to the beavers' woodyard.

He picked eight logs, each running close to eight inches thick and roughly eight feet long. He selected the driest ones he could find, going by feel. He'd learned that from firewood. The drier, the lighter.

The wood was soft, felt soft to the point of his knife, and he thought that might mean they would waterlog, but then he decided it wouldn't matter. It would take weeks, or at least days, to soak into an eight-inch log, and he wouldn't need the logs that long.

One way or the other, he thought, while dragging the first log down to the lake.

The beavers had left clear sliding trails where they had dragged branches down to the lake, and Brian used one of them, the main trail, to pull the logs down. The last four feet to the water were fairly steep and the mud was slick from the recent rain and the logs pretty much made their own way to the lake, pushing him ahead down into the water.

He had a plan – or as much of a plan as he could have for what he was going to try to do. He couldn't move Derek very far by mere strength – he had to weigh close to a hundred and eighty pounds, compared to Brian's one-forty. Brian couldn't carry him and could only drag him a short distance.

So he had to bring the raft to just below the shelter – bring the raft to Derek – and that meant building it here and working it up the side of the lake to Derek.

It took him less than an hour to get all the logs down to the water, and when he lay them side by side and lined the ends together he was pleased to see that they made a usable-looking raft. The ends weren't quite even, but close, and they were pointed, the way the beavers had chewed them off. It gave them a streamlined look.

Like something out of *Huckleberry Finn*, he thought.

Except that nothing held them together yet. Brian stood next to them in knee-deep water and studied the problem.

He had no rope, no string, and yet he had to have a way to hold the logs in a flat platform to keep them solid enough to carry Derek and him.

He had his clothing. His jacket – the same type wind-breaker he'd had when he first had to survive after the plane crash – and he had Derek's jacket as well, though Brian wanted to keep that for cover for Derek.

But even cutting the jackets in strips might not make enough roping to tie all the logs together. He cast around, half looking for vines or grasses he could weave into a rope.

But again the beavers helped him. They had also cut smaller sticks – limbs and the tops of the trees – some of them five or six feet long and two or three inches in diameter.

They provided his answer. He made cross-pieces with them, put one on top and one on the bottom and sandwiched the raft body logs in place. Then he cut strips from his jacket and tied the two cross-pieces together at the ends so that they were pulled together and held the logs firmly in place. By using his knife to notch the cross-

77

pieces to take the material, he made sure the cloth tie-downs didn't slip off.

He put four of these cross members down the length of the raft, tying them in place as tight as he could get them, and when he was done the raft was stout enough for him to stand on, jump on, walk back and forth on.

It was about eight feet long, five and a half feet wide, and floated well out of the water, and had not taken him more than two hours to build.

He had gone back twice to check on Derek while working and now that it was finished he cut a long pole for pushing the raft and used his knife to carve a crude paddle, then moved back to the camp before bringing the raft.

He was not hungry – still felt too nervous for hunger – but knew he should eat before they started or he would be too weak. So he ate nuts and some berries they had stored in a birch-bark cone, ate everything he could find in the shelter – they wouldn't need it on the run – and examined Derek closely one more time while he ate.

This whole thing, he knew, was crazy and had only a small chance of working. He knew that, understood that. If there was one thing he understood about working in an emergency – surviving – it was that there was a large measure of luck involved.

And if there was the slightest, tiniest change in Derek, any indication at all that he was coming out of it, Brian would call the trip off and hope for the best.

So he studied Derek, worked at it as hard as he could. He looked into the unconscious man's eyes and saw nothing, just the glazed look that was there before. He carefully measured his breathing and his heartbeat and found them to be the same – exactly – as they had been since he'd started to keep track of them.

He yelled into Derek's ear, looking for some reaction in the eyes, and there was no sign of any kind that he could hear, or that he could react to hearing.

Finally, he tried pain. He used the tip of his knife to poke Derek's hand, again watching the man's eyes and there was, simply, nothing – even when he poked hard enough to draw a small drop of blood.

No sign of any kind of life or knowledge except the breathing and the heartbeat.

Then he waited a few minutes and did it all again, working steadily, carefully, and it was the same. He had to be certain, absolutely certain that there was no choice.

And he was.

He stood and looked across the lake and felt strangely old. It was his decision to make and yet another man could die because of what he decided. He had never been in this position, and it frightened him. Even when he was in danger, even when he had to fight just to live, his decisions only affected him – never another person.

And now Derek lay there and Brian looked down to where he'd pulled the raft to the shore by the shelter and opened his mouth and said:

'We go.' It came out as a whisper.

Right or wrong, they had to do it – Brian had to do it. *Please, God*, he thought – and did not finish it. Just that – please, God. He turned to face Derek and coughed and said it again, loud and clear.

'We go.'

The River

SIXTEEN

It proved to be almost impossible to start.

Brian took the briefcase down to the raft, and decided to take a weapon – he left the bow but took two lances he had made. One fish spear with twin tines held open with a small stick that he had made to show Derek that you could use a spear as well as a bow to take small fish. The other was a straight spear with a fire-hardened point that he had decided to use if necessary on a moose.

'Did it really attack you?' Derek had asked, when he told of his time near the L-shaped lake and the moose attack. 'Really come at you?'

'And stayed with it,' Brian said. 'I couldn't do anything – it just kept coming back, pushing me down underwater until I pretended to be dead. Next time I'm going to fight back.'

So he had made the spear and hoped that he would never have to use it.

When the spears and the briefcase were on the raft, he went back to the camp.

Derek. The true reason for the raft. He had to get Derek down to the raft and on it without hurting him, or worse, drowning him.

He turned Derek on to his back, grabbed him under the shoulders, and tried to pull him down the bank.

Derek didn't move.

Brian pulled and the man just lay still, and Brian looked

to see if his shoe had caught on a root by the fire or in the brush, but it had not.

It just couldn't be that hard to move a – he almost thought body – person. Just a person on his back. He ought simply to skid down the bank.

In the end Brian did get him to skid – about three inches at a time. He heaved and jerked and pulled until finally Derek was on the bank, lying on his side, facing the water.

There was a small ledge and a drop of approximately six inches to the water. This close in to the shore the lake was very shallow, not enough water to float the raft, and Brian had to horse the raft sideways to get it in so that it was lying sideways next to Derek and just below him, grounded on the mud of the bottom.

He kneeled in the water next to the raft. He had been soaked since starting to build the raft and figured to remain wet until . . . until they made it. He did not wish to think of the alternatives.

He used his hip to jam the raft into the bank and reached across to pull Derek on to the raft.

Again, it was like moving lead weight. Derek seemed bolted to the earth and Brian had to settle for pulling first one end, then the other, back and forth from Derek's arms to his ankles until the man was at last on the raft, which settled into the mud of the bottom under Derek's weight and remained solid.

Brian positioned him first on his back and then decided he might choke and moved him over on to his side, in the centre of the raft. The middle cross-piece on the raft caught Derek in the soft part just above his hip and helped to hold him in place, but Brian did not think it would be enough. He tore more strips from his jacket and made a tie-down. This he used to go from one side of the raft, over Derek's shoulders to the other side, to tie him into position.

Finally, with Derek lashed in, Brian used Derek's own jacket rolled up to make a pillow, which he worked beneath Derek's head.

He checked the breathing and heartbeat again and he was surprised to see that he did it almost automatically. It had just been hours – just over a day and a half – and he was already reacting automatically.

'Derek, I don't know if you can hear me.' He settled in the water next to the grounded raft and spoke to Derek's face. 'I'm going to tell you anyway. We're going to take this raft down the river that leads from the lake. It's just under a hundred miles to a trading post. The thing is, we can't stay here because . . . well, it just wouldn't work. And the radio was blown by the same lightning that hit you. So we can't call for help. So we have to do this, we have to do this . . . ' He shook his head, choked, realised that he was close to crying. 'Oh, hell, we just have to do this – I hope it works out.'

He started to work the raft out of the mud and float it free when he thought of something.

What if they came unexpectedly?

If they just found Derek and Brian gone, they wouldn't know what to think.

He had to leave a note.

He opened the briefcase and took out a pencil and a notebook. He wrote in large, block letters.

> *Big storm.*
> *Derek hit by lightning and in coma.*
> *Trying to raft river down to*

Brannock's Trading Post 100 miles
south. Come quick.

BRIAN ROBESON

He studied the note, then added the date and time. He had left the radio behind back up in the campsite, thinking it would be in the way. He ran back up to the shelter and found the radio in its plastic case and folded the note and put it in the case so that it stuck out slightly. Then he tied the radio back up under the overhang with its carrying strap so that anybody coming into the shelter would be certain to see it.

Back at the raft he found that Derek's weight had pushed it into the bottom so hard, it was difficult to get loose.

He sawed it back and forth, one end out, then the other and finally it broke free, though floating still in little more than a foot of water.

'Good place to test it,' he said. It seemed very stable with just Derek on it and Brian carefully eased his knees on to the end by Derek's feet.

The end sank lower a few inches, but still was well above the surface. He raised on his knees and rocked back and forth, ready to jump off if it started over. The raft bobbed back to level and settled from the roll fast, the flat bottom slapping the water lightly.

'It's seaworthy.' He climbed back off the raft and checked Derek again. He was resting in the same position. Some water had come up between the logs and made his shoulders wet, but his head was up on the jacket pillow and was still dry.

Brian looked at the sun.

It was mid-afternoon. Dark was still five or six hours

away – not that it mattered. Once they started they would have to keep moving, even through the night if they could.

Time was everything.

The river left the lake at the south end, a good half mile away. Rather than try to move the raft across the lake, he decided to pull it around the edge in the shallows and he started moving along the shore.

The raft followed easily and Brian let himself feel just the slightest bit positive for the first time since the lightning had hit them.

The raft seemed to work well. The weather was holding. They had a map.

And most of all, Derek was still alive.

They had a shot at it.

SEVENTEEN

Their luck held.

Where the river left the lake it cut a deeper channel in the soft bottom. It took Brian half an hour to move the raft down the side of the lake, pulling it along by hand, and where the river exited he moved to the left shore and stopped for a moment.

One last thought. He could still go back. It would be easy to take the raft back around the lake, and possible – though certainly not easy – to drag Derek back up to the shelter. Once they were on the river, with the current, he would not be able to work back.

But he hesitated only a moment. Any choosing was already finished and he shook his head.

It was done.

He climbed on to the back of the raft, kneeling at Derek's feet as he had before, and used the pole to push it away from the bank and out into the current.

The river was sixty or seventy feet across, leaving the lake, and the current at the sides seemed a bit slower. It caught the raft and pulled the nose around, so it aimed downstream but along the edge, bouncing against the bank and sliding beneath overhanging willows and brush.

Brian used the pole – the bottom was four or five feet down – and pushed the raft sideways out into the centre.

It hesitated, seemed to hold for a moment as if trying

to find the current, then the moving water caught the logs and the raft started to move.

Inside of thirty feet it was matching the current, or close to it, and Brian watched the banks sliding past as the raft moved silently down the river.

'We're on the way,' he said to Derek. 'It's working and we're on the way.'

For a hundred yards the river moved straight, then curved hard to the left around a small hill where Brian quickly found that a log raft is not the same as a boat.

The current was not fast – as he had guessed earlier it was about the speed of a person walking – but it was steady and strong. The logs were heavy and once they were moving in a direction they were hard to turn.

As a matter of fact, Brian thought, watching the bank at the end of the curve come at him, they were impossible to turn.

The river curved left and the raft went straight, cut across the curve, and jammed into the bank.

The jar of the sudden stop, even moving slowly, rocked the raft and Derek rolled against the lashings and almost fell in.

Brian leaped forward on the raft, fell on Derek and held him while the raft lurched, slid sideways, and settled against the bank, where it stuck in the dirt and brush on the edge of the river.

One hundred yards and they were stopped.

Brian slid off the raft – waist deep in the water – pushed it sideways back out into the current, climbed back on and sat for half a minute while the river curved back around to the right and the raft jammed into the left bank.

Another fifty yards. One hundred and fifty yards and they were stuck twice.

Brian swore.

'I'm going to have to improve this or we'll be a month on this river.'

He worked the raft into the middle again and it started to move.

This time, as they came into a shallow curve and the raft started to move straight, he waited until the raft was close to the shore and used the pole to jam into the bottom and fend off.

He still shot wide on the turn, but they didn't jam into the bank and by the fifth curve he had found a way to use the crude paddle to steer the raft.

He would come in close to the shore on the inside of a curve, then as soon as the raft was around it he paddled the stern over and aimed it down the centre of the river, and fought to keep it in the middle.

They still did not always stay in the centre of the best-moving current, but as the afternoon wore on Brian found that by frantically paddling through each curve he kept the raft moving almost at the speed of the current and away from any brush or snags on the sides of the river.

It worked, but the river curved almost constantly, moving through small swamps and beneath overhanging trees so thick it seemed to be a jungle, and he was constantly fighting the raft.

Inside of three hours he felt his back and arms aching, and knew that if he didn't stop to rest a bit now and then he would never be able to make it.

He decided to stop every hour for ten minutes. Derek had told him once that that was what the military did on long marches – a ten-minute break every hour – and by the end of the fourth hour he was more than ready for it. As it happened the break came when the river straightened out, so he didn't lose any time. The raft kept sliding as he leaned back and rested his arms and back.

He used his hands to cup water into his face, rubbing the back of his neck. The evening sun was still hot when it hit him as they came out of the patches of shade made by the trees on the bank, and the cool water on his neck refreshed him.

'Let's see how we're doing.' He opened the briefcase and took out the map. The river was accurately drawn – or seemed to be – and as near as he could figure it they'd come about eight miles.

Not as good as he'd thought. Eight miles in four hours. Two miles an hour. That meant fifty hours.

Two full days, on top of the day they'd just used making the decision and getting ready to go. Four days without water for Derek.

He looked at the unconscious form and saw that the sun had burned his neck where the skin was exposed.

Well, if Derek couldn't drink, Brian could still keep him cool. That might help.

He took his T-shirt off and soaked it in the water. Brian used it as a cloth to wipe Derek's face and neck with cool water during his break.

This ordeal was amazing to him, and he wondered at how it could be. Things happened so fast, changed so fast. Derek had been – *no*, he thought – Derek *was still* one of those people who seemed so . . . so alive. He was eager to learn, happy, bright.

He seemed indestructible.

Even now, lying on his side on the raft in the evening

90

light – his chest rising and falling as he breathed – he looked like he would wake up any second.

Cut down – that's how Brian thought of him. He had read a history of the Civil War and the author had written about the men being 'cut down by fire.'

That's how Derek looked to Brian now – cut down. How could that be?

Here he was, no different really, had been in the same place at the same time and he was all right, and Derek was cut down.

He wiped Derek's face several times. All this time the raft had kept moving, and when his break was over he saw that they were coming into another bend.

He put the T-shirt back on, wet, and picked up the paddle and started to work, swinging the stern of the raft, keeping it in the middle of the current.

It would be dark in an hour or so, but he thought that it wouldn't matter. His hands were raw from the rough wood of the paddle and he thought that it wouldn't matter either.

All that mattered now was to keep moving.

EIGHTEEN

In the night, that first night, he learned some things about himself.

Not all of them were good.

He had not slept the night before except to doze kneeling next to Derek, and he had worked hard all day on the raft getting it ready, and when the sun went down and the darkness caught him he could not believe how much he wanted to sleep.

There was a partial moon – a sliver – which gave enough light to see the river, or at least make out the main channel, but the light didn't help.

Each time Brian's eyes closed to blink, they opened more slowly, and each time he had to fight to get them open.

The mosquitoes helped for a time. They came out in their clouds with darkness before the evening cool slowed them and Brian tried brushing them away from his face and Derek's, but it was like trying to brush smoke. As soon as his hands passed they settled again, whining in the darkness and after a bit he just let them eat and kept paddling.

Sleep would take him between strokes of the paddle; it would stop him so his arms would fall and the paddle would stop and lay in his lap. Then he would shake his head and snap out of it and start paddling again just in time to make a turn, at least at first. Halfway through the night nothing worked anymore and his eyes closed and stayed shut.

He dreamed mixes of things.

His mother came to him, sitting on the other end of the raft.

'It's all right,' she said. 'You can let go now – it's all right.'

And her voice was so soft, so gentle and soothing that he *wanted* to let all of it go, not to be here. Not even in the dream.

He was not sure how long he slept, but when he awakened the raft was drifting on a large, flat plain of water, bobbing sideways.

There was no sign of the river.

In the faint moonlight he could see no banks, knew no direction to travel.

'But . . . ' he said aloud. The sound of his voice startled some animal and there was a loud splashing to his right.

A large animal, he thought – perhaps a moose. That meant there was a shore, then, a bank for an animal to run on – close.

So use thought, use logic. Use it. Think.

The river was flowing generally southeast. It must have widened into a lake.

The moon.

The moon was straight overhead when he went to sleep. Now it was down a ways to the right.

Down to the west. Like the sun it rose in the east, set in the west.

The moon was about halfway down from overhead in the same direction as the splashing animal.

So.

Brian threw water in his face.

So the river had widened into a lake, but he had moved along the west bank. If he kept moving the raft with the paddle he should come to where the river narrowed again, and pick up the current.

He started paddling, the raft moving sluggishly now that there was no real current. He bore to the right, moving the raft sideways as he paddled until he could just make out the shoreline in the darkness – outlined in the moonlight – then he straightened and started paddling again, steady, reaching forward with each stroke, bending at the waist, two on the right, two on the left.

While the raft followed current well, because the logs stuck down into the water and were not streamlined, for the same reason it moved with the paddling horribly.

'It's like paddling a brushpile,' he said to Derek. 'Nothing seems to move.'

And in truth it was very slow. He was not moving more than a mile an hour and he wished he could read the map in the darkness. He didn't remember this lake, or wide place, or whatever it was, but if it was two miles long it would take two full hours at least to cross it.

Two on the left, two on the right.

He slogged forward and with the rhythm of the paddling his brain settled into numbness again and soon he was in the same trance that had led him to sleep.

This time he stayed awake, but the hallucinations grew more and more intense.

He saw the raft as a canoe and felt it fly forward with each stroke until he was leaving a wake of fire, firewaves curling out from the front of the raft and he worried that it would catch the logs/canoe on fire and burn them up and how could water be on fire anyway?

He would shake his head and then see his mother again at the other end of the raft. She would change into his father, who was smiling and beckoning him to paddle faster and faster; and then Derek's breath grew louder and louder until it filled his head, the lake, the world with the rasping sound of his breathing, and Brian could hear Derek's heart as well, pounding on the logs of the raft, echoing until all he could hear was the keening rasp of Derek's breath and the pounding of his heart . . .

He would shake his head and the raft would be jerking forward in the faint moonlight, Derek lying on his side, Brian leaning forward at the waist, two on the left, two on the right, the paddle pulling at the water in swirls. Three strokes, four, and he would be under again.

At one point something came swimming up alongside the raft – a muskrat or otter or beaver – cutting a *V* in the water as it swam next to Brian, and in a fraction of a second his mind had turned it into the head of some beast, some underwater monster with its toothed head weaving back and forth getting ready to attack, to sweep over and take him off the raft with huge teeth; and he set the paddle down and grabbed for the spear to kill the monster, make it go away before it could eat him, and he shook his head and the vision disappeared as the animal dived and the monster was gone and he was alone with Derek again. He picked up the paddle and worked again, leaning forward . . .

The bad thinking came sometime toward morning. He did not know how it started and would never know how it started and, later, did not wish to remember it when he did.

Two nights without sleep tore at him and the raft seemed bolted down as he tried to get it along the edge of the lake to where the river moved again. Somewhere there, as he tried to keep the raft moving and fought sleep, there came the idea, the wild idea, the sick idea.

The raft moved slowly because it was heavy. What made it heavy, sank it into the water so that it could not move, was the extra weight of the man tied in the middle. If the man were gone – if the man were gone it would be lighter and he could move fast and it would be better.

It would be better if Derek were gone. What was the difference? He was dumb enough to rise up and get hit by the lightning, and he should be gone.

Brian looked down at the still form and thought the thought; and it was so awful that he did not believe he was thinking it, but it was there, the thought.

If Derek were gone.

Just gone.

None of this would have happened if Derek weren't there – not any of it. And if Derek were gone . . . gone somehow in the water, gone down and down . . .

'No!' He nearly screamed it and the sound of his voice snapped him awake, alert, and he touched Derek's leg to make certain he was still there, that Brian hadn't cut him loose in the night and that he would always be there and that Brian would never even think the thought again. Not even for an instant.

'All the way,' he mumbled, reaching with the paddle again. 'We go all the way together.'

He paddled another half hour, fighting sleep and then at the same time he felt a coolness that he knew was morning coming and he saw that the eastern sky was beginning to lighten.

He stopped paddling, looked at the sky and was amazed at how fast the dawn came. One moment it was so dark he couldn't see Derek on the raft and the next he could make out the bank, see the trees in the grey light of dawn.

And they were moving.

The banks were moving along, even though he wasn't paddling. He'd done it, he was through the lake and had moved back on to the river and the current had him.

'Thank you,' he whispered, and realised when he said it that it was another kind of prayer and that he was grateful not just for the river, the current, the movement – but the other thing as well.

Coming through the night with Derek . . . grateful that he had made it.

'Thank you.'

NINETEEN

With the arrival of good light Brian took the map out and spread it on the briefcase.

The lake he had crossed did not show. He was positive. There were lakes, some large and small, but he was not moving fast enough to have reached any of them yet and that meant the map was not accurate.

It showed clean river with narrow banks where he guessed the lake to be and if it was inaccurate about this one thing then it might be wrong about all things.

Say the distance to the trading post. If the map had been made many years before and not updated, then the river might have changed direction, might not even go by the trading post any longer.

The trading post might not even be there.

The thought stunned him and he realised how foolish it had been to leave the lake and trust the map. There were so many variables, so many ways to go wrong.

He studied the map again and took some heart from it. It was so . . . so definite. It must be basically right. Close. Things could change, but not that much. The river was probably up a bit and the lake he had come through in the night was a low place that filled when the river ran high and not really a permanent lake that would be on the map.

Sure. There was logic there. All right. All he had to

do was test the map, find some way to ensure that it was mostly right.

He put his finger on the river and followed it, tracing the path as the blue line cut through the green, followed it to where he thought he must be.

There.

If the map was right and he was guessing right, he should be about where his finger had stopped. It showed a long straight stretch and the contour lines were spread far apart, which would indicate a large low or flat area where there might be a lake.

Better yet, in a short distance – less than two miles – the contour lines came closer and closer together and showed two hills, one on either side of the river, just after a sharp *S* turn.

The raft was moving well now and the morning sun was cutting away some of the ache and tiredness of the night. He put the map back in the briefcase and checked on Derek. His face was swollen from the mosquitoes in the night, his eyes puffy and shut, and Brian used his T-shirt to wipe cool water on Derek's face. He rinsed it in the river and dampened Derek's mouth with fresh, clean water.

He wasn't sure if his eyes were being tricked or if it was real, but Derek looked thinner to him and he wondered if getting thinner was a sign of dehydration.

He dampened the T-shirt once more and put it over Derek's head. If he stays cool, Brian thought, cool and moist, it might help. If I can keep him out of the sun . . .

If the raft had a canopy, a cover, it would help. He paddled to the shore and jammed the raft into some willows and grass. It took him a half hour to use some green willows and swatches of grass to arrange a crude awning over Derek. It did not cover the whole man, but kept most of him in shade, and when it was done Brian pushed the raft back out into the current and started moving again.

He watched for the hills. Hunger came with the morning and he started thinking about food. Cereal and milk, toast, bacon, fried eggs – the smells of breakfast seemed to hang over the raft.

It bothered him, but it was an old friend/enemy. He made himself quit thinking of food, thought instead of what to do, planning each move of the day.

Get a firm location, figure his speed, keep moving – a step at a time.

Time.

Time was so strange. It didn't mean anything, then it meant everything. It was like food. When he didn't have it he wanted it, when there was plenty of it he didn't care about it.

He stretched, sighed. 'You know, if we were in a canoe and had a lunch and a cooler full of pop, we'd think this was the most beautiful place in the world.'

And it was, he thought, truly beautiful. The trees, pines and spruce and cedars, towered so high they made the river seem to become narrow and in places where the bank was cut away by the moving water the trees had actually leaned out over the river until they were almost touching. They made the river seem like a soft, green tunnel.

The character of the river had changed. It happened almost suddenly, but with such a natural flow that Brian didn't notice it for a short time. The trees grew closer, the brush thicker and the banks higher.

Where they had been grassy and sloping away gradually, the banks were steeper and cut away, exposing the dirt and mud. The trees were so close and high that Brian would not be able to see the hills on the map when he came to them. He could see nothing but a wall of green.

He wiped Derek's face several times. All this time the raft had kept moving, and when his break was over he saw that they were coming into another bend.

He put the T-shirt back on, wet, and picked up the paddle and started to work, swinging the stern of the raft, keeping it in the middle of the current.

It would get hot soon and cook him, but he thought that it wouldn't matter. His hands were raw from the rough wood of the paddle and he thought that it wouldn't matter either.

All that mattered now was to keep moving.

TWENTY

He saw the hills from the map sooner than he thought he should see them.

But they were the right ones. He was sure of it. They rose steeply ahead and on either side, rounded but high, covered with trees.

It was just about noon and the sun was beating down on him. He reached under the shelter and used the damp T-shirt to cool Derek again.

'We're moving,' he said, his voice thick with exhaustion, not believing it. 'We're moving along now . . . '

And when he said it he knew it was true. The raft was increasing in speed. Even as he watched, the speed seemed to pick up.

'We're hauling . . . ' He started, then trailed off as it dawned on him.

The contour lines being close together on the map meant that the banks steepened between the hills.

If there were hills and steep banks, the river might drop, fall a bit.

He reached for the briefcase to take another look at the map, but stopped with his hand halfway out.

A sound.

Some sound was there that at first he could not place. It was so soft, he could almost not hear it at all over the sounds of the birds.

But there it was again. A hissing? Was that it?

No.

It was lower than that. Not to be heard, but felt.

A *whooshing* – water.

A water sound.

A rumbling sound. The sound of water moving fast, dropping, falling.

Falling water.

A waterfall.

They were heading for a waterfall!

TWENTY-ONE

There was no time left. The river had narrowed slightly, but now there was more of a drop and the speed had increased dramatically.

They were dead in the middle of the river and Brian knew he had to get to shore, had to stop, but there was no time.

Twice as fast as he could walk, the raft was fairly careening now.

The sound was louder.

If he tried to paddle for shore, he would succeed only in turning the raft sideways. He was not sure how he could get over a waterfall – if indeed he could at all – but he was fairly certain he did not want to try it with the raft sideways. If it went the long way over the waterfall, it would be harder to roll over. Sideways and it would roll easily.

The sound was a definite rumble now, and in seconds they wheeled around a bend and Brian could see it.

'God . . . '

It was a whisper.

It was not a waterfall, but it might as well have been.

The river moved between two large stone bluffs that formed the sides of the two hills Brian had seen on the map.

The bluffs forced the river to a narrower width, deeper,

and at the same time aimed it through some boulders that had split off either side and dropped in the middle.

All of this had the effect of making a monstrous chute where the water fought and roared to get through, smashing around the rocks in huge sprays of white water.

And the raft was aimed right down the middle of the chute.

Things happened so fast after that, there was not a way he could prepare for it.

The raft seemed to come alive, turn into a wild, crazy animal.

The front end took the river, swung down and into the current, grabbed the madness of the water and ran with it.

Brian had just time to look down at Derek, just time to see that he was still tied to the raft securely, and they were into it.

The raft bucked and tore at the water, slammed sideways. Brian tried to steer, using the paddle to swing the stern to the left and right, trying to avoid the boulders, but it was no use.

The water owned the raft, owned Derek, owned him. In the roaring, piling thunder of the river he had no control.

They were flying, the logs of the raft rearing out of the water on pressure ridges, slamming back down so hard it rattled his teeth.

In the middle of the chute was a boulder – huge, grey, wet with waves and spray – and the raft aimed directly at the centre of it.

He had time to scream – sound lost in the roar of water – and throw himself on Derek. The raft wheeled slightly to the left and struck the boulder.

Brian thought for part of a second that they had made it.

Derek's body lurched beneath him and dropped back, the raft took the blow, flexed, gave, but held together; and Brian started one clear thought: we made it.

Then it hit. There was an underwater boulder next to the giant in the middle of the river. Hidden by a pressure wave, it lay sideways out and to the left, halfway to the left wall.

The nose of the raft made it, carried over by the pressure ridge, hung for a second, then dropped, plummeted down.

As it tipped forward the rear of the raft cut down into the water and came against the submerged ledge.

'*Whunk!*'

Brian heard it hit, felt the impact and the sound through his whole body. He grabbed, tried to hold on to the logs beneath Derek, but it was no use.

The stern kicked off the ledge, slapped him up and away, clear of the raft, completely in the air.

He hung for a split instant in midair, looking down on the raft, on Derek – then he plunged down, down into the boiling, ripping water.

Everything was madness – frothy green bubbles, hissing, roiling water.

He came up for a moment, saw the raft shooting away downstream carrying Derek, then he was down again, mashed down and tumbled by the pressure wave, smashed into the rocks on the bottom, and all he could think was that he had to stay alive, had to get up, get air, get back to the raft.

But the wave was a great weight on him, a house on

him; the world was on him and he could not move up against it.

He fought and clawed against the rock, broke his face free, then was driven down again, hammered into the bottom.

Sideways.

He'd have to work sideways. Smashed, buffeted, he dragged himself to the side beneath the pressure wave.

It became stronger. He could not rise, could not get air, and his lungs seemed about to burst, demanded that he breathe, even if it was water. He willed the urge away, down, but it grew worse, and just when he knew it was over, when he would have to let the water in – when he would die – just then he made the edge of the pressure wave at the side of the boulder.

The current roared past the rock and took him like a chip, sucking him downstream.

He brought his head clear for one tearing breath, opened and shook water out of his eyes long enough to see that the raft was gone, out of sight – then he was driven back under, down to the bottom, smashing into boulders in a roaring green thunder, end over end until he knew nothing but the screaming need to breathe, to live, and then his head smashed into something explosively hard and he thought nothing at all.

TWENTY-TWO

Bright light flashed inside Brian's eyes – red and glaring – and he opened them to find that he was on his back, staring directly at the sun.

'*Ecchh!*' He rolled on to his stomach and spit and nearly choked on water.

He was in the shallows below the rapids, caught up in a small alcove in the shoreline.

The water was six or seven inches deep, with a gravel bottom. His senses returned and with them came the realisation that he was all right. He was bruised, but nothing was broken; he had taken a little water, but apparently had coughed it out.

He was all right.

Derek.

The word slammed into him. Somehow, he had forgotten . . .

He stood – his legs were a bit wobbly, but they held – and looked down the river.

It stretched away for half a mile, becoming more calm and peaceful as it dropped, nestled in trees and thick brush, a blue line in a green background. Birds flew across the water, ducks swam . . .

There was no raft.

Brian turned, stood dripping, looking upriver into the rapids.

From below they did not look as bad. The pressure

waves appeared smaller – even the boulder didn't seem as large. There was still the sound of the water – although that, too, was muted.

But there was no raft.

No Derek.

'Derek!'

He yelled, knowing it was futile.

He looked downriver again. There was no way the raft would have stopped in the rapids. It had to have come down, floated on downstream.

What had he seen? He frowned, trying to remember what had happened.

Oh, yes – the wave. The big submerged rock and the wave, the great wave had taken the raft and he had seen that – the raft moving off downriver. He did not think it had tipped; he seemed to remember that it was upright.

But Derek – was he still on the raft? He couldn't remember for certain, but it seemed that he was – everything was so confused. Tumbling in the rapids seemed to have shaken his brain loose.

He fought panic.

Things were – were what they were. If the raft rolled or if Derek fell off the raft, then . . . well then, that was it.

If not, Derek might still be all right.

'I have to figure he's still alive.'

And if Derek was still on the raft, still alive, he was downriver.

Brian had to catch him, catch the raft.

He started to move along the bank, and did well for fifty or so yards. The bottom was gravel – spilled out by the rapids – but then it ended.

The river moved rapidly back into flatter country,

swamps, lakes, and the first thing that happened was the bottom turned to mud.

Brian tried to move to the bank and run, but the brush was so thick and wild that it was like a jungle – grass, willows, and thick vines grabbed at him, holding him.

He moved back into the river – where the mud stopped him. If he tried to walk, when his weight came down, his feet sunk and just kept on going – two, three feet. The mud was so thick it pulled his right tennis shoe off, and when he groped to find it the mud held his arm, seemed to pull at him, tried to take him down.

He lost the shoe, clawed back to the bank and knew there was only one way to chase the raft.

'I'll have to swim.'

But how far?

It didn't matter, he thought – Derek was down there somewhere. Brian had to catch him.

He shook his head, took off his remaining shoe, and left it on the bank.

He kept his pants on – they were not so heavy – and entered the river, pushed away from the bank until he was far enough out to start floating a bit.

He kicked off the mud and began to swim. Within three strokes he knew how tired he was – his whole body felt weak and sore from the beating he'd taken in the rapids.

But he could not stop. He worked along the edge, half swimming, half pushing along with his feet in the mud.

Downriver.

He had to catch the raft.

TWENTY-THREE

He became something other than himself that afternoon.

When he began to swim – after he'd overcome the agony of starting and his muscles had loosened somewhat – he tried to think.

The raft would move with the current, if it did not get hung up.

Brian would also move with the current, plus he had the added speed of swimming, and he should gain rapidly.

But when he rounded that first bend and did not see the raft, and cleared the next bend two hundred yards further on and did not see the raft, worry took him.

He stopped at the side and stood as much as he could in the mud.

It was nearly a quarter of a mile to the next bend and there was no raft.

Every muscle in his body was on fire. He slipped back into the water and began swimming again, taking long, even strokes, kicking and pushing along the mud; pulling himself forward.

Another bend, and another, always reaching, and always Brian's eyes sought the still form, the thatched top of the raft.

Nothing.

The river seemed to have swallowed Derek. Altogether he rounded six shallow bends and still there was no raft, the stupid raft that had hung up on every bend when he was trying to steer it and now perversely held the centre of the river somehow. There was nothing but the green wall along either side, the trees that grew higher and higher now that the rock hills were passed, until they nearly closed over the top of the river; the green wall that closed in and covered him as he slid along the water, wanting to scream, but pulling instead, always pulling, a stroke, then another stroke, until there was not a difference between him and the water, until his skin was the water and the water was him, until he *was* the river and he came to the raft.

He nearly swam past it.

Brian moved near some willows, his face down in the water, reaching with his left arm and when he raised his head he was looking at the raft.

It had somehow come through all the bends and curves, and here must have caught a slight crosscurrent. The raft had moved to the outside of a shallow curve and had glided back beneath some overhanging willows and low trees.

All that showed was the rear end of the raft – and the bottom of Derek's shoes.

'Derek!'

Brian's hand had almost brushed the raft, but had he not looked up at the exact point that he had, he would have missed it.

He grabbed the raft, pulled himself up alongside.

Derek lay still, though his body had moved, twisted sideways on the raft.

'Derek,' he said again, softer.

Derek's head was still to the side, the eyes half open, but if he had been pushed underwater in the rapids, even for a moment, it might be too late.

112

'Derek.'

He looked done, gone, dead.

Brian tried his wrist, but could feel no pulse. He watched Derek's chest but it didn't seem to move. He leaned down put his ear against Derek's mouth, held his breath.

There.

Softly on his ear, a touch of breath – once, then again, small puffs of air.

'Derek.' He was alive, still alive.

It was as if everything came loose in Brian at the same time. His body, his mind, his soul were all exhausted and he fell across Derek, asleep or unconscious, fell with his legs still in the water.

'Derek.'

TWENTY-FOUR

Suddenly he was paddling.

His eyes were open and he was kneeling in back of Derek and he was leaning forward with the paddle and he did not have the slightest idea of how he'd come to be there.

He had a new paddle in his hands, carved roughly from a forked branch with a piece of Derek's pantleg pulled across the fork to form the face of the paddle. Brian was moving the raft and the sun was shining down on him and it was all, everything, completely new to him.

A different world.

'I must have slept, then moved in my sleep . . . '

The briefcase was gone – torn off in the rapids – and with it the map. Not that it mattered.

The banks were just all green and the river went ahead to the next bend. The trees hung over the top and there was nothing to see but a slot of sky and the water ahead and the endless, endless green.

Nothing to match with a map.

He could no longer think anyway. He had no idea how far they had come, how many hours or days they had been travelling or how far it still was to the trading post. He could only pull now, only pull with the paddle.

He knew absolutely nothing, except the raft and the paddle and his hands, which had gone beyond bleeding now and were sores that stuck to the shaft of the crude paddle; knew nothing but the need, the numbing, crushing need to get Derek somewhere, somewhere, somewhere down the river . . .

Food, hunger, home, distance, sleep, the agony of his body – none of it mattered anymore.

Only the reach.

The bend forward at the waist, the pull back with the arms, two on the left, two on the right.

Two left.

Two right.

Two.

Two.

Into that long day and that long night he moved the raft, so beyond thought now that even the hallucinations didn't come; nothing was there but the front of the raft, Derek, and the river.

The river.

Sometime in the morning of the next day, any day, a thousand days or eight days – he could not tell – somewhere in that morning the river widened and made a sweeping curve to the left, widened to half a mile or more, and he saw or thought he could see a building roof, a straight line in the trees that did not look natural and then he heard it, the sound of a dog barking – not a wolf or coyote, but a dog.

There was a small dock.

People had dogs that barked, and they had docks. He kept pulling, still not able to think or do anything but stroke, pulled to the edge of the river until the raft nudged against the docks, bounced, and then the paddle dropped.

He was done.

Above him on the bank he saw a small brown and white dog barking at him, its tail jerking with each bark, the hair of his back raised. As Brian watched, the round face of a young boy appeared next to the dog.

'Help. Help me,' Brian thought he said, but heard no sound. The face of the boy disappeared and in moments two more people came, a man and a woman, and they ran down to the dock and looked down at Brian and he was crying up at them, his torn hands hanging at his sides down in the water, down in the river.

The river.

'Derek . . . '

Hands took him then, hands pulled him on to the dock; and the man jumped in the water and untied Derek and took him as well.

Hands.

Strong hands to help.

It was over.

MEASUREMENTS

Brian, Derek, and the raft travelled one hundred and nineteen miles down a river with an average current speed of two miles an hour, in just under sixty-three hours.

When Brian started, the raft weighed approximately two hundred pounds, but soaking up water all the way, it nearly doubled its weight by the time they reached the trading post – which was actually nothing more than a small cabin on the river where trappers could bring their furs. The post was owned and manned by a husband, wife, and one small boy, but they had a good radio and could call for help.

Derek's coma was low grade, and in truth he probably would have been all right even if Brian had not made the run – although he would have suffered significantly from dehydration. He began to come out of the coma in another week and had fully recovered within six months.

During the run Brian lost twelve pounds, mostly in fluids, though he drank river water constantly to make up for it, and his hands became infected from bacteria in the water. He healed rapidly – his hands became amazingly tough – and strangely suffered no real long-range difficulties from the run down the river, probably because his earlier time – the Time – had taught him so well.

His mother and father vowed never to let him go in the woods again, but relented after some little time when

Brian pointed out that of all people who *were* qualified to be in the wilderness, he was certainly one of them.

About seven months after the incident, Brian was sitting alone at home wondering what to cook for dinner when the doorbell rang, and he opened the door to find a large truck parked in the street in front of the house.

'Brian Robeson?' the driver asked.

Brian nodded.

'Got some freight for you.'

The driver went to the rear of the truck, opened it, and pulled out a sixteen-foot Kevlar canoe, with paddles taped to the thwarts. It was a beautiful canoe, light and graceful, with gently curving lines that made it look wonderfully easy to paddle.

Written in gold letters on each side of the bow were the words:

THE RAFT

'It's from a man named Derek Holtzer,' the driver said, setting the canoe on the lawn. 'There's a note taped inside.'

He climbed back in the truck and drove away and Brian found the note.

'Next time,' he read aloud, 'it won't be so hard to paddle. Thanks.'

MILLIONS

by Frank Cottrell Boyce

Two boys.
One miracle.
A million chances.

When a bag stuffed full of money drops out of the sky
Damian and Anthony find themselves rich. Very rich indeed.
Suddenly the brothers can buy anything they want –
except the one thing they really need.

'Funny, direct and very often moving . . . It's hard
to imagine the person who wouldn't enjoy it'
Adèle Geras, *Guardian*

'Pure gold. Poignant and always entertaining,
Millions is magnificent storytelling'
Scotsman

'Charming . . . beautifully written'
Independent

'*Millions* is fresh, funny, touching and wise'
The Times

BOOTLEG

by Alex Shearer

The Good For You Party is running the country, and forcing
everyone to live healthier lives. Chocolate addicts Smudger and
Huntly watch in horror as their favourite food is swept from the
shops and Chocolate Trooper police arrest anyone caught with
sweets.

When the boys discover the recipe for making chocolate
and a hidden store of the right ingredients, they fight back.
Their secret bootleg operation is soon a brilliant success,
but how long can they keep selling illegal chocolate
before the Good For You thugs catch them?